BLACK LIGHTNING

ALSO BY ROGER MAIS

Face and Other Stories (1942)
And Most of All Man (1942)
The Hills Were Joyful Together (1953)
Brother Man (1954)
The Three Novels of Roger Mais (1966)
Listen, the Wind (Ed. Kenneth Ramchand, 1986)

BLACK LIGHTNING

ROGER MAIS

INTRODUCTION BY JACQUELINE BISHOP

AFTERWORD BY JEREMY POYNTING

PEEPAL TREE

First published in 1955
by Jonathan Cape
This new edition published in 2014
Peepal Tree Press Ltd
17 King's Avenue
Leeds LS6 1QS
England

Copyright © 1955, 2014 Estate of Roger Mais
Introduction © Jacqueline Bishop
Afterword © Jeremy Poynting

ISBN13: 9781845231019

All rights reserved
No part of this publication may be
reproduced or transmitted in any form
without permission

INTRODUCTION:

SURVIVING WHOLE

JACQUELINE BISHOP

1.

The woman wanted to know how I had done it.

"Done what?" I asked her, a little alarmed, searching my mind for what I could have possibly done wrong, for there was, it seemed to me, a slight accusation in her trembling voice. She was shorter than I was, older, and she leaned against a cane. I loved her name – Spirit – as much as I admired her warm brown complexion. She reminded me of my grandmother. The woman reached into her bag and pulled out a copy of my novel, *The River's Song*, encased in a transparent plastic covering, that she lovingly fingered.

"Rachel..." the woman said after a while, bringing me back to the moment, "I want to know how you knew all those things about Rachel..." she lowered her voice in the hushed sanctuary of the church. Service had only recently ended and several people were milling about. "...You know who I am talking about... the prostitute in your book."

The prostitute in my book.

I can't recall what I said to the woman, though I remember instinctively flinching, wondering if she thought that I was at one time, if not now, a prostitute, and that was why I was able to write the prostitute so well for her.

Tears started streaming down Spirit's face. "You see," Spirit said after a while, "at one point… at one point" she was searching for words, "at one point I was a prostitute." She stopped and searched my face again, no doubt looking for judgment, before she continued. "At one point, I was Rachel." She was having a hard time talking now and I was having a hard time concealing my surprise.

"I have carried that shame with me for a long long time," Spirit continued. "A long time now. But in this book… that Gloria [the narrator] loved Rachel, and it did not matter to Gloria what Rachel did or that she had been a prostitute. That little girl loved Rachel anyway. I wondered how you did that."

All I could tell Spirit was that I too love Rachel, that I was glad she chose me to tell her story, even as I marvelled that something that I created, or maybe I should say something that I helped bring into being, since I strongly believe that writing a novel is a conspiratorial thing between characters who choose authors to tell their stories and authors who take up the challenge, that a character in my book had moved from being among the pages of a book to forcefully enter someone else's life. The same thing had happened to me in the books I most loved, and I was humbled by the experience. I mentally thanked Rachel and all the other characters in *The River's Song* again.

My encounter with Spirit is probably the most memorable but certainly not the only encounter I have had, when I would come to the realization of just what it is that art can and should do; that the characters that one helped bring into being could be out in the world meeting and talking to other people. It would not be the first time that I would wonder about the role of the artist in society, and what responsibility the artist has to his or her creation. In time, as someone would come up to me after a reading, wondering where Gloria and Annie are these days, if they got reunited; or that time a niece of mine insisted that she knew exactly where the book was set – in Nonsuch, our maternal and ancestral home, high in the blue Portland mountains of Jamaica – in time I would wonder about the role of the reader in the artistic compact. Art is nothing, I eventually came to believe, if it is not a transaction.

Imagine then, my delight, when I started reading Roger Mais's amazing *Black Lightning* and realizing that it was precisely the very same questions about the role of the artist that I, as a barely begun artist, was asking myself, that Mais fully explored in this his triumphant third novel. I felt that I was simultaneously talking to and taking the hand of a father, an elder, an older brother, a friend even. The novel could not have arrived at a better time in my life.

II.

The outlines of the novel are well known: the protagonist, Jake, is a sculptor and blacksmith who is fascinated by the Biblical Samson as a symbol of man's independence, and of a man who is amongst strangers. Deciding to carve a mahogany tribute to Samson, however, becomes a more complicated affair when Jake's wife leaves him for another man and the issue of deception by a woman becomes more central to his thoughts. In the biblical story, Samson is of course blinded by the Philistines because of Delilah's treachery, and is left leaning on a young boy for support. In the novel, Jake is struck by lightning and left blind, forcing him to rely on his friends, particularly Amos, to survive. After leading him on a journey to discover just how reliant on humanity he really is, Jake's despair in his blindness ultimately drives him to suicide.

Those are the broad strokes.

But this is a novel that is concerned not only with the broad strokes, but increasingly with the smaller more delicate or intimate strokes. Time and time again in the novel the artist is positioned as the outsider, the one cursed or blessed, "to see for others what they cannot see for themselves", as I believe, the poet Adrienne Rich said. The issue of sight, sightlessness, insight and vision is invoked throughout the novel. The novel makes the point that even those with clear eyesight, and even insight, sometimes cannot see what is in front of them.

Take for example Mother Coby, a prophetess, who consistently exhorts Jake to repent his sins and cease making a "graven image" – the statue of Samson that Jake is carving out of mahogany. For Mother Coby, and too many people like her, the only creator is the almighty and to seek to be a creator is to equate one's self with the almighty.

Yet I find it hard to believe that in a Jamaica of tourist trinkets, indeed a Jamaica of pale-faced Christs in just about every church, that this is the first time that Mother Coby has been confronted with art-rendering. Yet Jake is the only person whom she chastises. So the question becomes: What is it that Jake is creating that is so bothersome to Mother Coby? For farsighted Jake, who rejects all the trappings of what his education could give him, to settle among his people and be a blacksmith and carver, the question is: what indeed would his carving look like? No doubt his creation is a reflection of the people around him, and it is perhaps this particular and local reflection that so bothers Mother Coby.

The difficulty that some have with the idea of artistic creation becomes even more evident when Jake is visited by his late father's friends Massa Butty and Tata Joe. These men, as representatives of the larger community, cannot understand why Jake, with all his good learning and education has settled into his father's old business of blacksmithing, and doing some carving on the side.

"I'm not trying to say it isn't a fine thing for a man to be able to do them things," Massa Butty says, "but what's it get you? That's what I'd like to know" (p. 81). This discussion exposes a significant ignorance as to who the artist is and what he contributes to his society. Neither men can appreciate Jake's art form or the struggle it takes to create art. This issue is further disclosed when Jake offers a gift to Tata Joe for Jake's goddaughter Esmeralda. While Jake is busy getting this gift both Tata Joe and Massa Butty say the gift is "Sure to be something that ain't a sight of good to anyone" (p. 82).

Again the reader is forced to ask, what indeed would "good art" look like to Massa Butty, Tata Joe and Mother Coby and what is it that makes Jake's art work so worthless? Whatever Massa Butty means by the pun embedded in his "ain't a sight of good" (it won't have any utility and it will offend the sight), the reader is forced to conclude that what Jake makes reflects something back to the society that members of the society have a hard time accepting.

Yet Jake, the artist, continues creating his work, knowing that it is as important for the artist to make the work as it is for the society around the artist to interpret and make sense of the work that is created. Indeed, for me, the novel gives one of the most moving descriptions of how an artist works: the intense concentration needed to create a body of work; how the artist is always alert to his vision slipping away; how the artist perhaps can see what nobody else can see. When Jake's helper, Miriam, for example, looks at what the artist has created she has sight but no vision, no matter how hard she tries to look. Miriam, like Mother Coby, is a representative of a society not sure about what they are looking at, or looking for – at what is coming into form. In so many ways these characters are a stand-in for a newly independent Jamaican society only beginning to imagine its future.

But if this novel details the hopes of the artist and does an admirable job of showing what it takes to make a satisfactory work of art, it also details the worst thing that can happen to an artist. Jake, as I have noted, loses his sight in a bizarre accident. Or is it, as Jake's estranged wife Estella insists, that Jake loses not just his eyesight, but his insight? In any case, the loss of but one of these two characteristics is detrimental to an artist. And, for me, this is ultimately why Jake decides to take his own life: he feels, having lost his vision, in the second sense, he has nothing more to contribute to his society. The question then becomes, if we take the physical loss as symbolic of the deeper loss of insight, why does Jake lose his vision?

In this novel the artist emerges as someone who questions his society, and does the supremely blasphemous thing in Jamaican society of questioning God. The novel shows us Jake's role as creator in a society that might not fully appreciate his creations even as Mais ruthlessly examines the role of the artist. It is fascinating the way in which this novel, published in 1955, anticipates some of the challenges that would take place in Jamaica in the coming years.

For example, in 1981, the sculptor Christopher Gonzalez heard that the Jamaican government was planning a sculpture in tribute to the late great reggae superstar Bob Marley, who had died in May of that year. Gonzalez submitted a winning bid to do the sculpture and turned in a rendition of Marley, with locks and feet curling into roots that seemed to be spreading out all over the world, which was vigorously rejected by the Jamaican government, the Marley family, even members of Marley's band. The public outrage was particularly vociferous and intense. As a child in Jamaica at the time I remember the furore of a large cross-section of Jamaican society (myself included) who felt that Gonzalez's work was a failure because it looked nothing like Marley. Who was this hallucinatory scary figure, eyes sinking into holes, I remembered thinking, that Gonzalez had offered us as Bob Marley? It was certainly not a Marley I could identify with then.

But in a strange kind of way Gonzalez's Marley stayed with me – much more so than the Bob Marley offered and accepted by another artist, the Marley that looked like Marley. Gonzalez's Marley was not a Marley that anyone could walk by without reacting to in one way or another. His was a Marley that caused people to stop and think. A Marley that was not obvious. A Marley that I carried inside me off the island, a Marley that informs my own work as a writer and visual artist these days. For I too wish to create work that make people stop and think. And this is what Mais's character Jake hoped to do as well in the art he created. He wished to get the people around him to stop and think.

Yet Gonzalez's story is a cautionary tale, for the artist, it is said, became embittered by this experience, and, for the most part, withdrew from making large-scale sculpture again. The public rejection hurt him deeply. He felt he had offered a gift to his people that had been promptly rejected. The artist Laura Facey faced a similar predicament in 2003 when her sculpture of a naked man and woman, which today graces the entrance of the Emancipation Park in Kingston, sparked intense and international discussion. Many felt that because of the artist's background (she is a white Jamaican identified with the upper class), she should not have been the one to land this emancipation commission. What could anyone of her background have to say about emancipation anyway? Weren't the vast majority of Jamaicans glad to be emancipated from people who looked exactly like Ms. Facey? These are some of the questions that Mais anticipated in *Black*

Lightning. As painful as they might be I still appreciate the furore that public sculptures can engender because it gives us a chance to discuss what a commission should look like and what responsibility, if any, the artist has to the people they are representing. Too often, however, the answers to the profound questions being asked are conservative, even reactionary. The Marley commission was eventually given to an artist who produced a work so like Marley that most people walk by it without actually seeing the work at all. Having us Jamaicans reflect on our troubled past, asking how the nation should be represented and who should do the representing, is an exercise we still need to encourage. This is what Mais's courageous book encourages us to do.

And then there is the question of what becomes of what the artist has created. Does the creation take on a life of its own as Jake seems to suggest? Does the artist become his creation? Or is the creation able to stand on its own? I want to believe that it is a little bit of both, that the creator is changed in the process of creation, and that the creation should be able to function on its own.

At the end of this novel, however, there is a tragedy. For Mais seems to suggest that his Jamaica has no use for the art created and the artist is forced to destroy his own creation. My hope is that this tragedy says more of Jamaican society in Mais's time than it does of Jamaica today.

For art to be art there has to be a transaction.

III.

In the story of Samson and Delilah, a good man is brought down by a bad woman. It is a theme that runs through all of Mais's published books.

It is a temptation to read the story of Samson as that of Jake, especially because of the parallels in the stories: Jake is seemingly betrayed by his wife in the same way that Samson was betrayed by Delilah. Both Samson and Jake end up blinded.

But the Samson and Delilah story acts as a foil for some of the larger questions that Mais is asking about Jamaican society.

For example, instead of heaping shame or scorn on Delilah,

Jake wonders why Delilah ultimately betrays Samson? What is missing from the Biblical account? A woman never betrays a man for money, Jake concludes, refuting the claim that Delilah betrayed Samson for however many pieces of silver. For a woman the betrayal most likely has to do with love. Perhaps, Jake thinks, all along Delilah had been in love with one of her own people. I appreciate so much this rereading of the Samson and Delilah story because it complicates who Delilah might have been. It makes Delilah a more noble character, a Judith who is concerned with the survival of her own people, as Mais, too, is concerned with the "survival whole" of his people.

The reader becomes aware that Jake, in thinking about Delilah's motives for leaving her husband, is thinking about his own situation, about why his wife, Estella, has left him for another man. It is the story that is not told. It would almost be palatable, even explainable, if she had left him for a man who has more money, but there is no evidence for this. More problematic no doubt for Jake is the realization that his wife left him not because maybe she loved someone else more, but because of a flaw in his own character. As Estella comments on Jake: "He lived by people's adulation, without even knowing it. Without it he was lost" (p. 161).

In so many ways Jake's estranged wife Estella, as a reformed Delilah, is one of the most arresting characters in the novel. Estella, like her husband, asks questions about the society around her; she takes risks, including risks with love, and at the end of the novel, pariah though she is, she is left standing while her husband decides to take his own life. Estella as an outcast, a woman who leaves a husband who was not abusing her, who still loves him, becomes a means to challenge woman's roles in the emergent Jamaican society, and for the society to know and understand itself some more. What is it, the novel seems to ask, that women will do in a new Jamaica? Estella's becoming a social worker after leaving Jake provides some answer to this question.

And then there is the role of an education in this society. Tata Joe and Mass Butty feels that Jake is "fit for better things" than to be a blacksmith "things that fit your kind of education." But Jake challenges their notion of what education should be and do, insisting that he "fixed old Mother Bado's bedspring... [and] her pains left her" (p. 80). The reader is left to ponder the question: What indeed is the role of an education if not to help with the suffering of those around you?

But maybe the biggest question that the novel poses is that of homosexuality in Jamaican society, as is expressed in the homoerotic tension between Jake and Amos. It seems to me that the Samson story of a man being betrayed by a woman is a creative foil in which to hide a homosexual love story for a society that might not have been prepared then, as too many are not prepared today, to face this love that dares not speak its name. Time and time again a subtle eroticism rises to the surface: Amos does not laugh when Jake suggests that he gets married; indeed with Jake, Amos is "like a patient dog waiting for his cue" (p. 39). Throughout the earlier part of the novel Amos is "meek" and receptive to Jake, assuming the stereotypically female role. Jake chides Amos about always being "so touchy" around him, while acknowledging that after all they are a couple of "queer ones", they are "kin", which is why they get along so well. Jake acknowledges that despite the fact that he treats Amos like dirt, still Amos keeps coming back.

At the beginning of the novel, Amos looks up at Jake "humbly", "imploringly", and gets upset that Jake is "still worrying about that woman" (his estranged wife). There are many moments of awkward silences between the two men. When other friends of Jake's, particularly men, drop by, Amos jealously slinks away. Furthermore, there is always eagerness in the voice of both men when they see each other.

Amos buys gifts for Jake "with my own money that I saved up – special for that purpose" (p. 105). The very air around Jake and Amos "seemed to be subtly charged with electricity... there was a kind of restless excitement in both of them" (p. 116). And when Jake is in one of his "black moods", "there wasn't no one but Amos could do anything with him" (p. 124). It is interesting to peruse why, despite the hinting at undeniable homoerotic desires, that this is never made explicit in the novel (though Jeremy Poynting's afterword argues that the theme can be teased out) – but then again this is a novel that is throughout rife with unrequited and frustrated love: Bess's love for Jake is not reciprocated; Estella leaves Jake for another man whom she eventually leaves as well; Bess cannot stand the feelings of love in her daughter that she recognizes in herself; then there is Glen and Miriam – Miriam who is always cutting herself in a symbolic representation of the hymen that refuses to be broken in her relationship with Glen.

IV.

The novel begins and ends in the woods where some of the most significant events take place. Readers of Thomas Hardy will note echoes in the prose of Hardy's pastoral under threat, *Under the Greenwood Tree* (1872), also a novel about art (in this case music – the novel is subtitled *A Rural Painting of the Dutch School*) and repressed desires. In *Black Lightning*, the woods emerge as a place of possibility, a refuge, a place of hiding and secrets, even as it is a place where love takes place. Estella meets her lover Steve in the woods, she also follows Jake into the woods on his way to killing himself, and she has a significant discussion with Amos in the woods that sheds light on aspects of Jake's character that are not readily available in any other part of the novel. In myth and folktale, strange and fantastic creatures inhabit woods, as strange and fantastic creatures inhabit the enclosed world of *Black Lightning*, an important novel that asks important questions of Jamaican society and anticipates some of the society's challenges in the years to come. What an absolute joy to have this novel back in print again.

BLACK LIGHTNING

ONE

Miriam walked deep into the wood, following the sound of the axe. Every now and then she stopped to scrape burrs from her dress, and then she would straighten up again, and listen for the sound.

The steady rhythm of the axe strokes was somehow satisfying, out here, deep in the wood, it went with the solitaire's treble fluting note in the distance, and with the sound the wind made going over the tree tops.

She came to a clearing, stopped, cupped her hand to her mouth, sang "*Yoo-hoo!*" twice; waited.

Nothing happened.

Only the steady axe strokes faltered, ceased altogether, and then started up again.

She set her lips tightly, and went on, deeper into the wood.

At last she came to the clearing where Glen was chopping firewood for the house. He knew that she was there, but he would not look up.

She sat down on a log, and waited for him to look at her, take notice of her, and speak first.

He was gathering up the split wood now into piles, tying them with withes. He straightened up to take the kinks out of his back. His gaze met hers, and he looked away.

She said: "I hollered, you didn't answer. What's the matter with you, are you trying to bear me malice?"

He came over to the fallen log where she was sitting, smoothing her skirt down with her hands. He stood looking down at her.

"Eh? Why you don't speak? What's matter, you bearing me malice?" she said, without looking up.

"Nothing is the matter with me that I know of. I thought it was you who didn't want to speak."

She looked up at him now.

"Well, aren't you going to sit down? I don't like you standing over me, talking down to me like that. I get a crick in my neck looking up."

He said, without changing his expression the least: "I guess I will sit when I want to."

She said, looking away, and picking at her skirt: "I know, you're vexed about last night."

He said nothing to that.

She said again, keeping her voice down low: "You should know I would have come if I could."

"Who's vexed? I wouldn't waste my time being vexed with a girl because she doesn't keep a date. There's plenty of girls who will."

"I know."

"Well then, stop talking nonsense."

Her lips trembled a little, but she held herself in.

"I had things to do. I couldn't come."

"I heard that before."

"You don't believe me. I know you don't."

"Well, why didn't you tell me that this morning?"

She looked up into his face now.

"Because you didn't wait to hear anything. You just went off into a rage."

He laughed. "Me! I was in a rage! Fancy that! I never was more calm in all my life."

"Yes. You were so calm I was afraid to say a word to you. I know that kind of calm," looking away again, "it is cruel and bitter like hate. This morning you hated me, and you had no call to."

"Why you say that?"

"You were just spoiling to pick a row. I couldn't say anything to you this morning to make you understand."

He said, bitterly, but relenting a little: "I know. I'm to blame for everything. I suppose it's my fault that you didn't come to the cotton tree, like you said you would."

She took a branch of dry twigs in her hands, started twisting them around, breaking off little pieces with her fingers.

In the distance the solitaire uttered his three melancholy notes, spacing them out, with a long interval between each. A woodpecker beat a rattling tattoo against a dry limb.

She looked down at the bundle of dry twigs in her hands.

"I am sorry, Glen. You were waiting long?"

His laughter sounded hard and mocking in her ear, made her wince.

"Don't worry," he said, "I didn't mind. I walked as far as the bridge…"

She shot at him quickly: "And you met someone?"

He said, off-hand: "Oh, some people passed."

"People –"

"I suppose it's my fault that you didn't come."

"I didn't say so." Her voice was little and held-in, and it didn't tell him what she felt at all. "Jake asked me to do something for him. That's all."

"You were down in the shop with Jake all that time?"

"No. He was working on his carving. I held the lantern for him."

He said gruffly: "Why couldn't he get someone else to do that?"

"I don't know. He is shy of people seeing his work before it's finished, I suppose."

She broke off a twig and put it between her lips. She bit little pieces off it from time to time. It had a bitter, stainy taste. She didn't mind.

Glen said, slowly, scuffing at the turf with his boot toe:

"He's not shy of you, though."

She looked at him now, shooting him a quick, straight glance, her head coming around sharply, so that she was looking across her shoulder, her face tilted up a little.

"What are you saying now? You're not jealous of Jake, are you? Oh, you couldn't be!"

"Oh no! I'm not jealous at all, you know that."

"Then why do you talk like that?"

"I suppose you didn't keep me waiting all that time. I suppose I ought to feel good about that." The wind went with the sound of continuous small surf in the tree tops over beyond them. Deep in the woods the pea-doves called to each other under their feeding trees.

Her gaze went back to the little bundle of twisted twigs she held in her hands. She said slowly:

"I don't understand people not being jealous. It don't seem to me natural."

"Well, I'm not jealous all the same. Maybe I'm not natural."

He tried to carry it off with a bravado, but the cruel, hard, artificial curl to his lips gave him away, and his nostrils quivered a little.

She said, without looking up:

"You wouldn't be jealous of Jake."

"And why not? If I wanted to be jealous of someone, why not him? Is he so different from other men? Answer me that."

The sudden vehemence in his voice assured her, made her feel instantly better inside her, made something like to laughter stir within her, but she kept her face very serious. She said, thoughtfully:

"I don't know. I just never imagined... oh, but you *couldn't* be jealous of him..."

His lower lip stuck out a little, the brown mood he was in giving itself away in his voice.

"But he keeps you in the workshop with him at night, where he won't let anybody else go."

"But can't you see, it's just on account of that why you shouldn't mind."

"Who says I mind?"

"I don't understand you. I don't believe you know what you are talking about yourself."

"I don't, don't I? Besides, why shouldn't I mind, if it comes to that? You tell me."

She let the twigs drop from her fingers, thoughtfully picked some burrs off her sleeve.

"Why don't you sit down? Aren't you tired of standing up?"

"I will sit down when I'm good and ready. Not before."

"All right."

A cloud drew over the face of the sun, and for an instant the wind died down. A lone pea-dove's call was a monody against the bright scherzo of afternoon.

"I wish you would try to be – reasonable," she said. "I don't believe you really – want me, at all."

"Now what are you talking about?" he said, in a different tone, sitting beside her on the log.

Her voice was low, he had to bring his face close to hers to hear her at all

"To hear the things you say, I don't believe you really..." a little catch came to her voice. "I don't know what to believe."

He wanted to make some gesture toward her, to put his arm around her shoulders, draw her close to him, but something held him. Instead he lashed himself further, and her, with his resentment that had stung him deep.

"I suppose you're still blaming *me* for what happened."

"Last night?" She shook her head. "No. But I want you to believe me."

"Well then you *do* believe?"

"I didn't say that either."

Her voice shook out a little warning of rising anger. She turned and faced him suddenly, bracing herself on the log behind her with one hand.

"Then what do you say? It must be one thing or the other. You make it so hard for me."

He said, out of the perversity that his mood had laid upon him: "Yes, I know, it is my fault," unwilling to give over.

Something gave a little in her own tension, she put out a hand and fingered a ravel on his sleeve, tentatively.

"Well, suppose you stop being so vexed-up about it?" she said, looking at her hand.

He said, after a moment's silence between them:

"Look, you have torn your apron."

She put a finger through the little rent. Looked at it. Laughed.

"Cho! It is nothing." She hesitated an instant, and plunged on: "You saw Violet, I suppose?"

He didn't say anything.

She went on, pursuing the thought that teased her mind: "She is always hanging around down by the bridge."

"You don't need to worry about Violet, she's nothing to me."

"Was she there?"

He reached down, picked up a stone, flung it into the branches of a tree.

"Well?"

"I'm not saying she wasn't; what I'm telling you is you don't have to worry your head about anything like that."

"I'm not worrying." She looked away, down at the log beside her, broke off a piece of stripping bark. "If you want her, I'm not going to hold you."

He said, harshly, "I don't want Violet, you know that."

The cloud passed from under the sun, and the russet tones of the middle distance were changed back to bright orange again. From far away came the sound of an accordion.

She said, slowly, breaking to pieces the dry bark between her fingers, and throwing them away from her piece by piece:

"Yes, but what about her. She wants any man she can lay her hands on." Turning toward him quickly, "You know it is true."

He didn't answer her question that was more like a challenge than anything. He brought his hand up from resting on his knee, touched her on the arm lightly.

"Where you get that from?"

"Eh?"

"This here."

"Oh, I got a burn."

"I can see that. It is blistered. But how you got it?"

"From the lantern. It was an accident."

He didn't say anything for a while.

And then he said: "Oh."

"I got tired, and it wobbled. And the shade was hot."

He said again: "Oh." Like that.

Nothing more.

She said, pursuing her own thoughts: "Poor Luther."

He said, almost savagely, "What's the matter with him? What you want to be sorry for him for?"

"Nothing."

He looked away again.

"You don't want to be worrying about Luther nothing. He can take care of himself."

"Not where it comes to Violet, he can't."

"If he's got any sense he'd know how to settle her."

"Maybe he hasn't got that kind of sense. He's jealous."

She gave him a quick, sidelong glance; but it had gone past him, as though he hadn't heard.

He said, nodding his head at her, his lower lip beginning to jut a little: "One of these nights it's going fall on you, perhaps, and set you on fire, next. That'd be a nice thing to happen; you'd like that!"

"What are you talking about at all?"

"The lantern that you have to hold for him while he does his precious carving. Why can't somebody else do that for a change, and why he have to work at night, that's what I'd like to know."

The sound of the accordion, carried on the wind, came to them more plainly, a melancholy tune.

"That's Amos, up by the sugar mill. He'll be coming this way no doubt. He takes this short cut every day to the village."

But he wasn't to be put off.

"Why he have to work at night, eh?" he pressed her. "You answer me that – if you can."

"You gone back to that again?"

"Yes. Why not?"

She looked at him keenly; trying not to laugh in his face, wanting to breach what lay between them, rather than otherwise.

"If I didn't know you better, I'd think you was jealous yourself," she said, quietly. He had no answer to this, and after a bit she said, again: "But you shouldn't be jealous of Jake."

"No more should you be jealous of Violet!" he flashed at her.

"That's different," she said, slowly, her gaze going away from him again. "I know Violet."

"What's the difference? I suppose you don't like him?"

"Jake? Of course I do. Everybody loves him. But that's different."

He repeated after her, slowly, thoughtfully: "Everybody loves him... Not Estella, though."

She turned on him quickly: "Why you should say that?"

"I fancy there is something going on right now, and it's not so good, the way I have it figured out in my mind."

She was silent, looking down at her hands in her lap.

He went on, as though he hadn't noticed anything: "You mind

you don't get mixed-up in it, all you do. You better watch your step, if you know what's good."

"You shouldn't talk like that," she said, in a low voice. "You know Jake just worships the ground she walks on." She laughed shortly. "It's funny, though!"

"You don't like her – very much, eh?"

"It's not that."

"What then?"

"I think she's making him unhappy. She has no right to do that."

"Nobody hadn't ought to make anyone else unhappy – like that," he said, looking at her closely.

The sound of the accordion came to them, sobbing on the wind; it grew in volume, and then receded, as the wind freshened and strengthened and held and died down.

"He's miles too good for her, anyway," she said. "She doesn't understand him."

"What do you know about that?"

"I know. I've got eyes in my head."

She broke off, and said again, in a different voice: "Anybody can see what I seen."

"You better mind what you say."

"Why? She is walking out with that stranger from the lowlands. Don't everybody know it, excepting he?"

"He comes from her district. She knew him a long time back. How do you know there is something between them?"

"People are too deceitful."

"Yes, indeed."

"And some never seem to be satisfied."

"Right again."

"Look at her. You would think – " She broke off again, and finished: "There isn't a finer man in all the world."

They fell into a kind of reverie, and there was silence, except for the sounds that went on in the wood – the wind going through the trees, the plaintive calls of the pea-doves, the swell and ebb of the accordion playing up at the mill-yard.

It was he, at length, who broke the silence between them.

He said, earnestly: "Jake is all right. It's a pity if it's true."

She drew a little closer to him.

"You're not vexed anymore?"

"I waited for you – "

"Yes, yes. I know. I'm sorry, Glen. Next time Jake asks me – "

His arm went around her shoulders.

"Don't say it, Miriam. We've got to stand by him, got to help him. Now more than ever. He needs it. He's a fine man."

"I'm so glad to hear you say that."

"You think I'm so low I don't know a fine man when I see one, eh?"

"It's not that at all. Sometimes I believe – "

"Believe what?"

"Never mind. Let's not talk about anything like that now."

She put her head down on his shoulder, and they fell silent again, listening to the sounds in the wood all around them.

He drew her closer to him, until she was lying across his knees, his arm supporting her. His other hand was employed urgently, otherwise.

Waves of pleasant heat fanned through their bodies, until she whispered: "No, Glen, wait. There's always people walking through this wood."

But he was impatient, tried to still her fears, her little anxieties, all the holding-back that was instinct in her. Still she whispered: "No. No. Wait."

She put her two arms up, and around his neck, drew his face down to hers, set her lips against his hard, trying to still the tumult that trembled through them.

She lay with her head across his arm.

Presently a little shudder went through her.

"The wind is blowing chill. You feel cold," he said.

"I'm not though. Glen…"

"Eh? What?"

"This evening at dusk…?"

"Down by the bridge? I'll wait for you."

"There'll be a moon, and all."

"You should have seen her last night. She was a witch."

"Tonight she'll be even better – you bet."

"Supposing he wants you to hold the lantern for him to-night?"

"I'll be there. I'll be waiting for you."

The accordion music sounded suddenly very close, as though they had not heard its approach for the other things that claimed their whole attention, until now it was so close.

She came upright quickly, pulling down her dress.

"It's Amos. He often comes through the wood," he said.

"Don't want him catch me here."

She went running lightly toward the little brush the other side of the clearing.

He turned from looking after her and walked slowly to where he had left his axe.

2

Amos came to a part of the wood where two tracks crossed. He sat down on a big moss-covered stone, took his accordion in his hands, started to play a mournful tune.

He played until he came to the end of that tune, then he started at the beginning and played it all over again.

He put the accordion down on the grass beside him, slapped a woodland mosquito that had settled on his neck, reached into his back pocket, brought out the makings, started to roll himself a cigarette.

Someone was coming toward him through the wood, he could hear the snapping of twigs under feet. His face made a grimace of irritation. He started to get up, thought better of it, shrugged his resignation, settled himself again on the stone.

A woman's voice hollered, "*Miriam!*" And hollered it three times, altogether, with listening pauses between.

And after that the wood went silent again, except for the low cooing of the pea-doves, and the distant sound of an axe. The axe-sounds broke off for a bit after the voice hollered the first time, and then they started up again, and didn't stop after that. They were slow, regular strokes, one coming after the other, spaced out evenly, forming a rhythm of their own.

Amos smoked in silence, sitting there like he was a part of the stone. The woman came on muttering and crackling through the brush. When she caught sight of Amos she came straight over to where he sat. He gave her a scowling, sidelong look, but she didn't pay it any mind.

She was a stout woman, and she stood before him now, panting hard.

"Bless my soul," she said, puffing out her cheeks. And then she said, "You seen Miriam? Been looking for her all over."

"Ain't seen nobody," he said, looking around him. "Nobody at all."

He clicked his teeth, and tried to look straight through her, pretending she wasn't there.

"What's the matter with you? What you so huffy about?"

"Nothing, Bess. Just ain't seen nobody, that's all."

Bess stood with her hands planted on her hips. Her gaze went over his head, in the direction from which the sound of the axe was coming. She kissed her teeth, shook her head.

"What these young girls are coming to, I don't know."

"You wouldn't," he said.

"Eh? I wasn't talking to you, Amos. Where's you' manners, anyway?"

He paid no attention to that. He pulled a grass straw, and stuck it between his teeth, his eyes looking everywhere but at her.

"The risks they run, the young girls of today," Bess went rambling on, talking aloud to herself. "When I was her age I would like to see myself running off into the wood alone, any old time of the day, and meeting young men."

"You weren't ever a girl, don't tell me," he said.

She turned upon him, wrathfully:

"Amos Gladstone, I don't want any of your lip today. I got just about as much as I can bear."

He chewed a piece off the grass straw, spat it out.

"All I say is, if you was ever a girl, then I was your sweetheart."

"Don't you talk to me like that, Amos Gladstone," she said, getting on her dignity immediately, her fists planted firmly against her broad hips. "You talk to me like that, I box your headside for you. I don't come here to hold-up any conversation with you, anyway."

"Well, all I say is, she ain't here. There's nobody here, as you can see for yourself. Do you think I'm hidin' her, or something?"

He went on chewing at the grass straw, his head deliberately averted, trying to give her a hint.

But she passed it up.

She said: "This wood here is as much mine as it is yours. I'll have you to understand I can come here as I please, and stay just as long as I please, without asking your leave. You old *curmudgeon*!"

He spat again and said: "The wood ain't mine more than it is yours, all the same a man has a right to be alone, who come so far to find it."

She looked at him, blinked her eyes.

"Find what?"

He shifted on the stone, turning the other side of his face to her.

"Never mind what. If I was to tell you you wouldn't understand."

And he added after a pause.

"There ain't nobody here. You can see that for yourself."

Bess opened her mouth to say something, and then the wind blew the sound of the axe strongly this way, and she closed it tight as a trap. She nodded her head slowly. And then the sound of the axe ceased altogether. Her lips tightened some more.

Her head bobbed up and down, and her expression was deep and knowing.

Amos looked at her now, his ugly face creased into a malicious smile. He nodded his head to keep time with her.

"So there," he said.

Bess gathered up her skirt, got ready to launch herself on the last leg of her journey.

She threw a glance at him over her shoulder.

"Jake's looking for you," she said.

He said, dully: "You lie, I just left Jake."

She laughed.

"So-long then, Old Misfortune!"

He looked up at the trees above him.

"Old cow. Old she-ass. Old scratch-cocoa," he said.

He continued, in the same even tone, as though speaking to himself, saying his thoughts out loud:

"No wonder the poor man had to die to leave her. Couldn't get rid of her no other way, I guess."

Bess gathered her skirt close against her plump legs, continued to walk away with as much dignity as she could command.

"As though anyone would want to stop and talk with *you*!" she said.

He looked after her, made a face, shouted: "Old cow-itch!"

He bent over, took his accordion in his hands again, made on it a soft note or two, stopped, shouted again, louder still: "Hogwiss!" But she took no notice.

He laid the accordion on the grass beside him again, settled himself in a new position on the stone.

He heard people talking, coming down the track. A man and a woman. He got up, gathered his accordion under his arm, went slinking away quickly, noiselessly, in the opposite direction.

His shoulders were hunched, throwing his head forward a little, and with one leg a good inch shorter than the other, he went with a limp.

"People thick as trees in the wood. Can't go nowheres now, for people. Blast them!" he muttered, as he went slinking, noiseless as a shadow through the trees.

3

A woman and a man came and stood in the little clearing where the two tracks crossed.

The woman said, coming to a stop beside the stone Amos had just quitted: "We can talk here safely."

The man moved nearer to her, a step, made a gesture toward her with his hands.

"Estella, you've got to listen to me."

"I'm trying not to, Steve," she said, her fingers clasping themselves into knots before her. "I want to listen to my conscience, only you – you won't let me."

He started to make a movement toward her, stopped short.

"You want me to go away, then?"

"I heard you were planning to leave – suddenly like. I wanted to see you before you went – for good."

He looked down at the ground before him, kicked at a loose stone.

"You would have seen me. I wasn't planning to go without seeing you first. You ought to know that."

Her fingers made themselves into nervous knots in front of her bosom again.

"I am not sure about anything, anymore. Not about myself, or anyone. I don't believe in people anymore, like I used to."

He said, bitterly, still looking down at his feet: "You mean, you don't trust me."

"No, not that, either. Don't trust myself, would be more like."

He turned suddenly, came nearer to her a step, as though to take her in his arms. She put her hands out, as though to hold him off.

"One thing you ought to be sure of by this," he said, "you can't go on living with him any longer. You don't love him, that's why. It's me you love."

"No, Steve, don't rush me. Give me time to make up my mind."

He laughed, harshly: "It's made already. You're just stalling, that's what."

She made a half-about turn.

"Not that, Steve. I've got beyond that now."

He laughed like that again.

"You tell yourself things. You try – "

Something choked him. He swallowed hard.

"He's a fine man, Steve. You never would know how fine a man he is."

"You love him? Is that what you're telling me?"

Her fingers made themselves into knots again.

"I wish I knew. I wish it was as simple as that."

He said, doggedly: "It's me you love. You're just trying to fool yourself. But you can't fool me. If I was to go away tonight, and leave you here without a word, you'd be sorry."

She took her lower lip between her teeth, and let it go.

She looked at him hard.

"You won't do that. You can't frighten me."

But he was tough. The brute-thing in him asserted itself. He would hurt her now, without pity. He laughed.

"Won't I? Well just wait and see."

She said, slowly, her voice toneless, flat: "I know. You're a brute. You could do anything."

He said, doggedly: "I love you." And that was all.

She turned away from him again.

"Don't talk to me of love. What do you understand about love."

"I understand it a man's way. It's him, or me; you've got to make up your mind, that's all."

She said, suddenly, tensely: "If he should find you here, now, he'd kill you."

He laughed again, like that: "You think so?"

"Don't laugh. I know it. What's more, you know it."

"All right, I won't laugh. So he would kill me... so then what? What would happen to you after that?"

His tone grew harsh, mocking.

"All right, he's a great big hero, an' all. But happens it's *me* you love, see? So what's the difference, I ask you? Oh, why can't you have some sense about it? Do you have to act like this all the time with me?"

"I'm not – "

He cut in quickly: "Yes, you are. You're just acting all the time, and I'm tired of it."

"Go on, Steve, get it all said, and be done."

"You want to make sure, yes. But it's not anything like what you're handing me. What you want to make sure about is that I don't go back on you."

"I hadn't even thought of that. You are a brute, you know."

He laughed, knowing that he had hit her hard. He was like that, all the way through. But he was something other, too. She knew it, and knowing it, all it meant to her, could forgive him this.

He said, changing his tone now: "I love you, see?"

She just shook her head, looking straight at him.

"I do. That's on the level, and you know it. But if you want it so, I'll leave you here tonight, and not say another word."

She saw that he meant it. He wasn't bluffing.

"Yes," she said, "it is you I love." Saying it slowly, dully, like a child saying its lesson aloud.

Her hands clenched into tight fists.

"And why shouldn't I? Don't I have a right to – to my own life at all?"

She took a deep breath, held it, then let it go.

"All right, Steve, go… go quickly… before I change my mind."

He took her by the wrist, jerked her round to face him.

"You mean it?"

She nodded, "Yes."

"I don't get you. Somehow I don't believe you're acting now. Estella…"

She looked at him, meeting his gaze steadily.

"I said, go."

He let go of her wrist, laughed, a short, tight laugh.

"All right, I'm going. But get this, you'll be sorry; you wait and see."

"If ever I am, I'll come after you."

He said: "Estella…" and stopped short.

He shook his head. Something within him urged the stupidity of all this.

"Look," he said, "I'm not going to let you send me marching like that. After all, I've got a stake in this."

She said, a little woodenly, like she was repeating a lesson she had learned by heart out of a book: "If anyone has a right to – to anything, it is he."

"Don't make me laugh. That's Sunday school stuff. You don't owe him anything. You don't even believe it yourself."

"He has given me everything…"

He said, brutally: "It's me, or him you love?"

"Don't let's go back again – "

"The late bus leaves at eight. I know the driver. I can make him wait till a quarter past. You got all your life before you."

"He needs me. My life is here. He's worth ten like you and me, together."

"Good God! To hear you talk – "

"He needs me, that is all."

He said, bitterly: "You learned your lesson well in Sunday school, didn't you!"

He laughed: "You're kidding yourself. You're just telling yourself that because there's nothing left for you to hang on to. You know he doesn't love you, really. It's himself he loves. He's just wrapped up in *that*! You know it. You've told me as much yourself."

"Perhaps you're right. I'm kidding myself – maybe. But it's not him anymore, or me. It's the things he can do."

"Christ! you make me sick. Look here, look at me."

Suddenly he took a quick step toward her, pulled her into his arms. She tried to fight him off, pleading in a strangled sort of voice, "Let me alone… I must think… think…"

He pressed his mouth to hers, making an end of her pleading, held his mouth pressed against hers until she stopped thrusting at him with her hands.

Then he broke away, laughed.

"All right, you can get on with your thinking now. I know – what I know… and that's all I wanted to know."

He turned, still laughing, started to walk away quickly, stopped.

"The bus leaves at eight o'clock. By a quarter after it will be going by the bridge, you will hear it blow coming around by Long Common Corner."

He turned and walked away, without looking back.

She crouched down, rather than sat, on the stone at her feet, tried to sort out the confusion of her thoughts. She could hear the sound of an accordion going away in the distance, after a few minutes, and again the steady, rhythmic song of the axe.

She lay over on her side, pressed her hand into it as though she was taken with a cramp. She turned over, and lay on her belly, still.

She stretched out her arms above her head, and her fingers clutched at the tufts of scrubby grass that grew there, and tore at them.

And then she lay still.

The sound of the pea-doves calling to each other under the sweetwood trees, the song of the axe, the wind soughing through the branches, were the only sounds in the wood.

A shudder passed through her. She turned over on her side

again, sat up, pressed her fist into it, bending over, as though taken with pain.

The first brown smudgings of dusk shook out over the silent wood. She stood up, looked about her, as though she had lost her way, turned and went stumbling down the track that went to the edge of the wood, where it met the common beyond, this side of the house.

4

Jake, too, came a walk into the wood.

He was looking for Amos; had heard he had gone that way. He had closed the blacksmith's shop, things were slow just now; left it to the boy, George, to lock up.

He was a very big man, tall and powerfully built. He went along with an easy swinging stride. The sound of the accordion led him to Amos. He found him squatting under a bastard-cedar tree.

Amos stopped playing when Jake came up, but Jake, squatting down beside him, nodded his head and said: "Play, man, play."

Amos took up the accordion again, and made it sob mournfully between his hands. And when he came to the end of the piece he was playing, he looked earnestly up into Jake's face.

"You like that one?" he said.

"Sure. Sure. Play another."

But Amos hesitated. He laid the accordion aside.

His monkey's-face of cocoa-brown became suddenly twisted as with pain. He screwed up his eyes, looking sideways at Jake.

"You know somep'n, Jake," he said, and broke off suddenly.

Jake smiled.

"Well, what's it?" he said. "What you got on your mind, pardner?"

"Oh, nothing, Jake."

"Must be something, pardner, you can tell me."

"I forget."

Jake laughed.

"All right," he said. "What about a bit of music instead, eh?"

"Don't feel like it," said Amos, huffily, "it don't sweet me anymore."

"What, the music don't?" Jake shook his head, looking down at the ground between his knees. "Sure must be something bad on your mind, pardner, to make you feel like that. No mind, come up to the house and have a bite of supper with me, eh?"

"Well, Jake, as a matter of fact – "

But Jake just held up his hand.

"Look, I'm not going to take any excuses tonight," he said. "I'm tired of you making excuses every time I ask you up to the house."

"It's not that, Jake, honest. It's this way – "

"I don't care what kind of a way it is. Look, I'm asking you for the last time, come on up to the house and eat a bite of supper with me."

"All right, Jake."

Jake looked at him, and Amos looked away.

"That's right, pardner. I sure feel better now."

"It's not I don't want to go up to the house with you,' said Amos, stumbling for words. "Not that at all."

"Suppose we just forget it?" said Jake.

"All right, Jake. We'll just forget it, if you say so."

"That's fine."

"It's Estella – " he began again, and broke off.

"Yeh, I know, you and Estella don't hit it off too well together. I know all about that. But it's just because you don't each give the other a chance. I want that my friends should like my wife. I want that you two should know each other better. You get what I mean?"

"We done knowed each other, all right," Amos grumbled, pulling a grass straw and sticking it between his teeth. He chewed on it like a rabbit, his squat nose twitching in the middle of his face.

Jake, looking at him, laughed. Amos gave him a scowl.

"It's all right," he said. "You can laugh."

"Wasn't laughing at you, pardner. Just laughing, that's all."

"Well, anyway you can laugh, but I wouldn't take it from anybody else, see?"

"You mean it like that?"

"Yes, I do."

"What would you do, pardner, if, like you say, somebody else was to take it into his head to laugh at you?"

"I'd up and spit in his face."

This time Jake put his hands behind him, to hold himself up, he was laughing so hard.

Amos looked at him, his ugly face working.

Suddenly Jake stopped laughing.

"Sorry, pardner," he said.

Amos looked at him, and spat out a piece of grass straw. He didn't say anything, just went on chewing, his jaw muscles working quickly, his nose jumping in the middle of his face.

"Sorry," said Jake, again, "I wasn't laughing at you, all the same. Just a picture like come into my mind. You're a funny cuss, Amos. But I like you. You know somep'n? You got guts, that's what. I like a man with guts. You don't lean on anyone, you don't need anyone help you. You're on your own."

"What you mean? Everybody's on their own."

Jake shook his head.

"Not the way I see it, pardner. Everybody's holding on, leaning on the next."

"That's the way it was meant to be, I guess."

"You think so?"

"Yeh, that's how people come together in the world, and do things between them, like. You follow?"

"Yes. I follow you. I'm wondering, that's all."

"Well, how else do you figure it should be? Awe hell, Jake, it's best the way it is. Just leave it be."

"Nothing else I can do about it, pardner. Come on, let's you and me take a walk up to the house."

5

They sat on the veranda after supper and smoked and talked.

Estella had excused herself earlier. Said she had a headache, she was turning in for the night.

"You see what I mean?" said Amos.

"Awe, forget it!" said Jake.

His voice sounded irritable, mean. He couldn't bear to be crossed and, when it happened, even in little things, he always got like that.

But presently it passed, and he felt sorry for the way he had answered Amos, so he tried to turn it into a joke now.

He said: "Seems I'll have to fix it so you get married, Amos. You never will learn to understand women otherwise."

Amos didn't laugh.

"Awe, forget it!" said Jake, even more irritably now.

He said suddenly, offering Amos his tobacco pouch: "You want to smoke?"

Amos took the proffered tobacco pouch without saying anything. He reached a rice-paper out of his pocket, rolled himself a cigarette, lit up, leaned his head against the railing, blew smoke through his nostrils, his eyes half-closed.

Jake slowly wadded tobacco in his pipe.

"I been thinking," said Amos, presently, breaking the silence.

"Eh?"

"I been thinking, kinda turning it over in me mind. You know that piece of field you got behind the stable, where the land slopes away?"

"Yes. What about it?"

"You could terrace that bit of field and make a slap-up vegetable garden out of it. With all the manure that comes down from the stable to it, would grow things a-wonder, I'm telling you."

"Yeh," said Jake, getting his pipe going.

He put his feet up on the veranda railing before him, leaned back comfortably in his chair.

He said: "Maybe she does have a headache, you never can tell."

"Eh? What's that you say?"

"Oh, nothing," said Jake.

He puffed his pipe in silence. Talk went stale between them, and nothing gave.

6

Glen, going past Bess's cottage down the road, heard the old dun cow mooing softly. Something moved him to take a look over the hedge.

He saw the old dun cow licking a newborn calf under a guango tree.

"Well, bless my soul!" he said.

He thought the old dun cow was too far gone in years to calve again. Thought it was just her belly swelled, like Bess's belly had swelled on her from years coming on, and from eating too much. And there she had gone and done it!

Well, wouldn't Bess be glad!

She would be still up at the house washing up after supper, he guessed.

He looked up, and there was the moon coming up over the hill.

He could picture the bridge in his mind, whitewashed all over like new with bright moonlight.

Well, Bess would soon find out for herself, anyway.

Now there was a thrifty cow for an old woman to have!

You couldn't go wrong with cows.

That's all a man needed to make himself into somebody. A few acres of land, a bit of home, and a cow.

He wondered – just wondered – if she would be at the bridge already, when he got there.

No need to hurry, now. Take his own time.

Never seen the moon so bright, far back as he could recollect.

He didn't see the figure a little way up the road that suddenly skipped over the hedge by the common, crouched down behind the bushes until he had passed.

He was walking along slowly, his hands deep in his pockets, staring, lost, up at the moon.

When he came near to the bridge, he put two fingers between his teeth, whistled loud, a single blast.

He saw a slight figure move from under the shadow of a tree just across the bridge, and come walking slowly toward him.

Felt like something stopped working inside him an instant, and then went racing along. He took his hands from his pockets, and same time quickened his pace. He walked the next twenty yards like that, scarcely setting his feet down on the road at all, and there was a wild singing in his blood.

7

The two men sat on the veranda and smoked in silence, until presently Amos said: "Something wrong to hell with it all!" As though he was speaking aloud his thoughts that had surged up out of all that mess of thinking, to the surface of his mind.

"Eh? What's that you say?" said Jake, like a man coming awake out of a dream.

"What I say is a man should amount to something in the world."

"M-m-m," said Jake, and went back to his own thoughts again.

"Every man should amount to something, yes, else what's the sense being born."

"Yes," said Jake.

He removed the pipe from his mouth, gently knocked out the charred tobacco from the bowl against the veranda railing, laid the still warm bowl against his cheek, gently rubbing it up and down.

"What's eating you now?" he said.

"Thinking," said Amos, "that's all."

"Sometimes a man thinks too much. Too much thinking not good all the time."

"Times a man gets thinking – 'bout life, an' things – he just can't stop himself, I guess."

"Yes," said Jake. "Well, what about it? You got any new ideas?"

"Hell, no."

"You see what I mean."

"Guess I better be pushing on home," said Amos, coming to his feet.

But Jake said, quickly, "No, sit awhile."

Amos sat down again, obediently, looked across at Jake like a patient dog waiting for his cue.

"It's a lovely night for a walk," said Jake.

"Yes, for them as like walking."

"Don't you like walking, Amos?"

"Well, it gets me around."

"Like that, eh?"

"Yes, about it."

Jake said: "Smoke?"

Amos hesitated.

"Go on, help yourself, man."

Amos reached for the tobacco pouch.

The mare, Beauty, whinnied from the stable across the yard. Sound of Bess singing, washing up the supper things in the kitchen.

Amos grunted. "Some people can't sing for peanuts, they croak like a frog."

"What's Bess done you now?" Jake laughed.

"Done me nothing a-tall. You think I should like the way she sings?"

"Well, pardner, we can't all be nightingales, you know."

"Nightingale, nothing! Even an old cling-cling could make a pleasanter noise than that she doing."

Again Jake laughed.

Anyway it was something to have the old scratch-patch around. Well, sometimes.

The mare over in the stable whinnied again.

Amos held up a hand, listening.

He said: "Now, that's a sound."

"You mean she sings better than Bess, eh? Maybe you got something there, pardner."

"Maybe nothing. Compared with *her*, that mare can *sing*."

Jake laughed, pulled his feet down off the veranda railing. Got up.

"Well, if you're ready I'll walk you home."

"No need for that, Jake. I can see meself home, I'm used to it."

"It's a fine night," said Jake, "think I'd like a stroll."

"If you'll wait for me I'll just go inside and change me boots," he said.

And Amos said: "Okay."

Amos sat on the veranda and waited what seemed to him like a long time, before Jake came back from the room.

He looked like a man who had seen a ghost. He tottered a little as he walked.

He stood holding a piece of paper in his hand.

Amos came to his feet instantly.

"What's the matter, Jake?"

He started to shake his head, changed his mind half way through the first motions.

"She's gone," he said, like that.

"Gone? Who? Man what you talking about?"

But even while he said the words he knew perfectly well what it was.

TWO

It was evening, and the blacksmith's shop was closed, and Glen, his day's work finished at the shop where he assisted Jake, was up at the stable grooming down Beauty the mare.

George, a boy going on fourteen, who helped down at the blacksmith's shop, and made himself generally useful about the yard, if not in fact, at least in intention, was sitting in the feed trough chewing a stick of sugar-cane.

Beauty wasn't taking too kindly to Glen's grooming, and every now and then she kicked out viciously, seeming just to miss him on purpose, or else she laid her ears back and made a pass at nipping him on the arm.

And Glen wasn't paying much mind to her antics, knew there was no real wickedness in her to speak of, and he was thinking his own thoughts.

The analogy between the mare and Miriam was too obvious to escape his attention. Both were high-spirited, young, full of life, full of little perversities and contradictions such as one didn't seem able to get at the bottom of, or properly understand at all.

Beauty now, he thought, hadn't been backed for three months. Not since the day the woman had run away. Jake, who used to love taking her out for a canter, just didn't bother with such things any more.

Without even stopping to think about it one could arrive at some reasonable excuse for Beauty's behaviour. But Miriam, now... Oh well, it wasn't from lack of work or exercise she suffered, Bess more than saw to that.

The comparison went teasing through his mind, and any conclusions he might have arrived at didn't seem to help him any at all.

Well, anyway, women were contrary creatures, he thought, and considered it best, for the present, to leave it at that.

His thoughts turned to Jake.

Now there was a man had got himself messed up proper by a woman, he thought.

Jake was never the same since Estella run away from his home that night, and the difference wasn't something you could just put your finger on and say it is this or it is that; it was something other, and more.

George, chewing away on his stick of sugar-cane, and spitting out the trash he had chewed up, all over the place, didn't contribute anything to Glen's peace of mind, or to the quiet operation of his thought-processes, because he kept fidgeting up and down, like a little monkey all over.

Now he would be squatting in the feed trough and, before you knew it, he was swinging from one of the rafters that held up the thatch on the roof. No sooner had you got him down off that than he had found him some new devilment or other to pursue.

He said now, grinning cheekily at Glen: "Cho! no' mind me, son, girls are all the same." He spat out a piece of chewed-up cane pith, dragged his sleeve across his mouth, bit another piece of juicy pith out of the sugar-cane, and said, chewing on it all the time: "They got fowl feathers in their brains."

"What you know about it?" said Glen.

"Bwoy, I know plenty! One time I used to have a girl."

"You don't say!"

"I left her out after a while though. They don't take nothing serious. They worse than jigger-fleas for jumping around."

"Lissen, supposin' you just get down out of that feed box and cut you' braggin' man-talk?"

"All right, feller, take it easy now. Who is braggin'? Bwoy, you just don't know nutt'n at all."

Beauty, becoming ticklish at the curry comb against the tender part of her belly, aimed a tentative kick at Glen's leg that just missed him by an inch.

"Next time she don't miss you, perhaps, young fillies and gals is all the same. Hm! you better watch out, bwoy!"

Glen brought the curry comb to rest on Beauty's rump, looked thoughtfully across at George and said: "The way you talk force-ripe, anyone would think you knew something about it, what month you born in, eh?"

"I was born April the first, didn't you know!" said George proudly. "Teacher Dawson and Alexander the Great and me."

"Who him?"

"Which? Alexander the Great? Bwoy which cow-pasture you was settin' springe in when them sent you to school?"

"I wasn't setting springe in any cow-pasture, and if you don't know who Alexander the Great is, I could tell you."

"Well, supposin' you tell me then?"

"Why, don't you know?"

"He was a great general, if you want to know."

"You not telling me nothing, boy!"

But George swung the talk away from Alexander the Great, and brought it round to more immediate matters.

He said, shaking a finger at Glen: "You make a gal get sassy with you, and she get away with it, bwoy you can't hold her at all."

"What you talking about, anyway?"

"You take the gal I was friendly with, she up and sass me one day, I slap her down."

"Mean to tell me you slapped a girl?"

"Yeh, why not?"

"You ought to be ashamed of yourself. I wouldn't talk it if I were you."

"Ashamed of meself, what you sayin' any at all? I'd be ashamed of meself, yes, if I had a gal could make me chase meself around in little circles. You bet I'd be ashamed."

Glen reached for a loose rope-end that was hanging out of one corner of the feed trough, but before he could employ it to any useful purpose, George had scrambled like a monkey up to the rafters, and he just clung there.

"Come on down," said Glen, swinging the rope at him.

He just grinned down at him.

"Nothing doing, bwoy, I like it fine up here."

Beauty put her head around just then and took a nip at Glen's arm. It wasn't a hard nip, but it made him jump, and shout at her: "Here Beauty! Behave, now! Whoa!'

George found the scene extremely diverting, he laughed so hard he almost let go.

2

Up at the house Jake was having supper, and Bess was serving him. But tonight, as usual these past months, he had little appetite, little zest for his food. And she fussed over him, as though she blamed herself secretly that he lacked interest in the meals she cooked for him.

The fact of the matter was she was working up for herself a nice case of nervous indigestion without knowing it.

She put her hand before her mouth to stifle a belch now, but in spite of every effort on her part, it announced itself.

She said: "Pardon."

He looked up from his plate and said, "Eh?"

"It's the gas," she said, "it gets on my chest, and I don't know what to do for it."

He said: "Oh!"

"I am sure I have tried everything for it," she said. "But nothing give me any relief at all."

He just looked up from poking the food around on his plate, set his fork down, leaned back.

"Goodness gracious!" she said, "but you haven't scarcely touched anything."

She was greatly distressed, what with him not eating anything scarcely, and the burning in her chest, and all.

"I don't feel very hungry," he said. "Nothing the matter with your cooking, Bess."

He gave her a wan smile and was on the point of pushing back his chair, but she put out a hand quickly, and it was almost as though she was going to push him back into it.

She said: "For goodness sake! You not finished already? Surely! And I have cooked you, as a special treat, a lovely mock-apple pie!"

The distress in her voice was more than he could withstand.

He reached way down inside him for a smile, got his face

started on it, said: "Well Bess, let's see what you got, eh? Bring on the pie."

She burped again, and went from the room quickly, without even stopping to ask pardon, lest he should change his mind.

She came back from the kitchen, bearing triumphantly before her a golden-brown pie.

She set it down before him.

"I made it with cho-cho, it tastes just like apple, the real thing, cinnamon an' all."

"I am sure it is going to be just fine, Bess," he said, giving her the rest of that smile.

He helped himself to a portion, and was carrying the first forkful to his mouth. Halfway there he paused, his hand arrested in the process of transferring it to his mouth.

She started to fuss immediately, with deep concern.

"Goodness gracious, what's the matter now? Don't it just smell nice?"

"Er, yes. But, am, I don't think I – feel very hungry, Bess, if you don't mind."

He set down the fork on the plate again, and she came near and bent over it.

"Goodness gracious!" she said, putting her hands up to her head. "How did *that* get in there!"

"It must have flown in through the window while you were fixing it. It's on account of you make it so nice not even the wasps outside can resist it. Don't worry about it, Bess."

She said: "A wasp! Now in gracious name, how did *that* get in there."

She clutched at her apron, brought it up to her face.

He said again, "Please don't worry about it, Bess." He rose, and took her arm. Gently pulled her hand away from her face. Saw that she was crying.

3

When Glen came around to the kitchen from the stable he found Miriam and George seated on the step, laughing and chatting together. She was seated on one tread of the step, and he on another below her. It sounded as though he was giving her jokes, and George cut short in the middle of what he was saying, as Glen came around the corner.

He was turning over in his mind whether he should stop or walk on, but something happened to decide his actions for him.

They both started to laugh.

It commenced as a tight sort of giggle at first, and then it went up and up, and presently they were both rocking on the step with laughter.

Glen felt suddenly hot behind the ears. He stopped dead, turned and faced them. He had no clear picture in his mind of what he was going to do.

He just lunged forward and made a grab at George.

But George, as quick as anything, sprang to his feet, and started running away, carrying his laughter with him.

Not stopping to think why he was doing it, Glen started to chase him.

He chased him like that up and down the yard space in front of the house, and between there and the woodshed.

George tripped as he was trying to slip under Glen's arm over against the woodshed, and Glen just reached down and grabbed him and pulled him to his feet.

He unbuckled his belt with the other hand. Without a word he went to work on George, belting him properly.

He knew that he had hurt George hard, in his sudden, uncontrollable rage.

And just as suddenly he felt ashamed of himself. He let go of George, who had both arms flung up about his head, fending off the blows which were raining down upon him every-which-way. He let go of George like that, and George sat down hard on the ground.

But the anger in Glen had not burned itself out.

He realized all of a sudden that it was not George he wanted to give a good belting to, but Miriam.

He turned and walked over to where she sat now, his anger against her burning inside him a hot, bright flame.

He walked right over to where she sat on the step and suddenly she stood up facing him.

He came and stood right close up to her, so that he could have touched her by reaching out an arm. But he only looked at her with that hot flame of anger burning through him, and said nothing at all.

Without taking his eyes off her face, breathing heavily from his exertion, he slipped the heavy leather belt around his waist, buckled it in front, gave a hitch to his pants, turned, and walked stiffly away.

4

Amos dropped in after supper for a chat.

Jake and he sat on the veranda and smoked.

The night was dry and hot, and every now and then there was a flicker of lightning in the sky. And after the lick of lightning, a bit, there was a heavy roll of thunder from far away.

"I have a feeling," said Amos, "we going to have a storm or something soon."

"Yes," said Jake.

"Don't like how the air is, kind of heavy, thick, and warm. Feel as if you can scarcely pull it into your lungs, you know that way?"

"Yes," said Jake.

"If it's not one goddam thing it's another," said Amos.

And Jake said "Yes," again.

And after that Amos was silent for a while.

Presently he got up to go.

"Why you going already?" said Jake.

"Well, I guess you just don't feel too much like talking tonight, Jake," he said.

"Who said I didn't feel like talking? Talk, man. I want to talk."

"All right, Jake," said Amos, taking his seat again.

He passed his hand across his face, and it came away sticky.

"Hot as Jesus, tonight," he said.

"Don't swear man." said Jake.

"Sorry," said Amos. "Just slips out, don't know why."

"Yes, it is kind of hot and close tonight," said Jake. "Feels as though it's going to storm."

Way out east they could see fork-lightning streaking down the sky. They sat in silence, it seemed a long time, waiting unconsciously for the following roll of thunder.

Presently it came, muffled, and far away.

"It's storming now, already, I bet, over there," said Amos.

Jake didn't say anything.

Presently:

"You ever see lightning like that without thunder?" said Jake.

"What you mean?" said Amos.

"You ever see fork-lightning like that without thunder?" Jake said again.

And Amos hesitated a bit, and said: "No."

"Old people have a saying if you see lightning without thunder like that, it means the lightning has struck you, and you're probably dead." Jake laughed a little, "Funny idea that, eh?"

"Not so funny," said Amos. "'Pends on how you look at it, I guess."

"It's funny any way you look at it," said Jake.

"What's so funny about it?" said Amos.

"You'd be lying there dead, and not even know it. That's kind of funny, if you get what I mean."

Amos shifted his weight on the chair.

"Don't like to hear you talk like that, man," he said, "you gimme the creeps."

"You scared of death, Amos?"

"Don't know, Jake, I never thought about it. No, man, I never give it any thought."

"You ought to," said Jake.

"Eh?"

"Every man ought to think about two things, sometime or other, life and death. Those two."

"Jesus! To, hear you talk sometimes! You gimme the creeps."

"You scared of death, that's what. You shouldn't ought to be."

"I don't know, Jake. I just don't ever stop and think about it, that's all."

"Well, you should."

"What you mean?"

"Everybody should, that's what I mean."

49

"I don't like it too much when you get morbid like this, Jake."

"What, you want to talk about something else? It's okay by me."

But Amos was silent, brooding over what Jake had said.

"I don't too like how you get that morbid sometimes, Jake," he said.

Jake laughed.

"I thought you wasn't going to talk about that any more? Let's talk about the weather, man. It's going to storm."

"It ain't healthy, like," said Amos. "A man shouldn't brood too much over – over things, I say."

"Who's brooding? Don't talk foolishness, if you don't have nothing to say."

And Amos just sat back, cowed, as though he had struck him across the face.

Jake suddenly felt irritable. With Amos, himself – mostly with himself for letting go at Amos like that.

He wanted to say, "I'm sorry, Amos," and erase it, but instead he said: "A man thinks about things, you call it brooding. I should just make things go through me like a dose of salts, and get nowhere, like some."

Amos just shrank in his chair, seemed to grow littler and littler, and it was like another goad to Jake.

"Why don't you say something? Why you just sit there?"

Amos stirred uneasily in his chair. He made a desperate effort to think of something to say, but nothing gave in the gaping void of blankness that went on above his ears.

He cleared his throat. Twice.

And suddenly Jake laughed.

"It's all right," he said. "Don't start your piles bleeding, man, just sit back and relax."

And Amos joined in the little joke at his expense, laughing longer than the other, but he wasn't enjoying it too much.

Presently Jake said: "You better stay the night. Might start raining any time now."

Amos got up then.

"No, Jake, I think I can make it."

"Don't be a fool, man," said Jake.

"All right, Jake, if you want it."

"If I want it nothing, can't you see it's going to rain like hell in a minute?"

And Amos said, meekly:

"All right, Jake."

5

The next day and the next Glen did not come near the house, and as it was he who always split the firewood for the kitchen, Bess was considerably put out. In her fussy, blundering way she kept poking over this irritation, and Miriam got in the way.

"They are all alike," she grumbled, "they are only around when there is something to be got. Good-for-nothing bunch, the lot of them, I say."

"He's not like that at all, Ma," said Miriam, instantly.

Bess just stood still for a moment, glaring at her, her mouth gaping a little.

"Gal, you stand there contradicting me! What you know 'bout it, at all? You must be want me fire you a box side of you' face!"

Miriam just shrugged, and turned away.

Bess saw the gesture, read in it a certain assertiveness that she was not prepared to let pass like that. She set her lips together tightly.

"Come here," she said.

Miriam came up to her obediently, looking her squarely in the eye, instead of hanging her head before her, looking down at her feet.

This to Bess was an act of overt defiance. Her own daughter! Things had come to a pass, indeed! It was time she took a hand.

"What you have with him?" she demanded, coldly, grimly.

"What you mean?"

"Don't back-answer me like that. I asked you a question, like I have a right to. You watch you' step, and answer me good."

"I don't understand you, Ma," said Miriam.

"I'm asking what he mean to you, that's what."

"Don't mean nothing special, like so, Ma." She added, bitterly, and with sufficient cause, "We're not even friends."

Bess shook an admonishing finger in her face.

"You better watch your step. You just a young gal, I want you to know. You make me catch any young man playing any hanky-panky with you."

Miriam's gaze faltered before her now, her lower lip jerked a little, and she held it between her teeth to keep it still.

"All right, you get on with what I gave you to do now," said Bess, feeling as though she had discharged her obligations as a parent, clearing up a little issue that was in doubt, as Miriam turned away.

6

He had lately taken to reading the Bible. He was not a deeply religious man, just about average for those parts. That is to say he went to church about one Sunday in every month, paid his dues, and the other days conducted himself in a normal, civilized way.

He was particularly attached to the story of Samson. He had read it over many times, turning it over in his mind, meditating on it; thinking over the causes and issues of his life, and what must have gone on under the surface between himself and Delilah. Things that the Bible never mentioned at all. Things other than, and more complex, and in a way more disturbing than what was discovered in the bald account.

And this was not to be wondered at, seeing that the big carving he was engaged on just then, and had been working on for the past several months, was a life-size statue of Samson. He was carving it out of a solid block of mahogany. He worked in a kind of loft above the blacksmith's shop. Evenings he worked, after the shop was closed, and even at nights, sometimes.

They had knocked off for lunch now, and Glen and the lad George had gone a walk down by the river, and he was left alone in the shop.

After he had eaten his lunch, he wiped his sleeve across his lips, sat down on a bench over by the window and opened the Bible.

He thought now that the biggest thing in the story was not

Samson's betrayal by Delilah, not the fact itself, but what must have secretly lain underneath, and had gone before, that the Bible never gave any clue of at all.

A woman, he thought, betrayed a man not for silver, but for love.

Was Delilah in love with one of her own people, one of the Philistines? Obviously she was attracted to Samson in the first place on account of his great strength, his virility. But he had not lost that. He was a man in the full prime of his manly inheritance of strength and vigour when she betrayed him and brought him to his great humiliation at the hands of his enemies, and to his death.

So he pondered these matters, and shook his head over them, and at last laid the Bible aside.

And then he went over by the furnace where the great anvil was. He bent down and took up the heavy sledgehammer, and felt the weight of it in his hand.

Suddenly he swung it up above his head with both hands and brought it down on the anvil a resounding blow.

And the head of the hammer flew off, like a stone from a sling, and it made a hole clean through the opposite wall, and lodged some ten paces away in the soft turf.

And he was left holding the haft only in his hands.

7

George was demonstrating to Glen, down by the river, how he caught crayfish with his hands alone.

He took off his clothes and got into the water, keeping to the shallows at the side of the stream. He bent down and carefully inserted his hand under a stone, and then went on to another and another, like that. Until presently his hand under the stone gave a little jerk, his face went kind of anxious for a moment, then a wide grin spread over it and he straightened up holding a flipping crayfish in his hand.

It was not a very big one, and Glen was inclined to be a trifle scornful.

"Cho!" he said, "that little janger don't even hatch good yet."

"What you know? This one is a swell-paw, they never grow much bigger than this. Only in the claw, one of them keeps on growing and growing, and the older he gets the bigger it grows."

"Hm!" said Glen, "you know any more good ones like that?"

"It's the gospel truth," said George, he made the sign of the cross across his chest, "cross me heart and may I die!"

"Oh, you swearin' now!" said Glen.

"Not swearin', man. You call that swearin'? Cho! I could swear good, mek you hear, you would know the difference, bwoy!"

"No need," said Glen. "I guess I heard all them words before."

With a *whoop!* George dived into the water. He swam around a bit at the bottom of the pool. He came up, spouting water like a porpoise.

The sluggish water made little ripples where it flowed over some submerged rocks on the other side.

"You catch any more of them little jangers?" said Glen.

"Wait, bwoy, I'll bring you up an old conger-eel next time."

"Conger-eels don't grow in little rivers, they grow in the sea," said Glen.

And George said, "Bwoy, you don't know nutt'n 'tall, old conger-eel he commence a pickney in the river, he get bigger an' bigger he swim right out to sea."

He took another header into the water, and swam around the bottom of the pool some more.

Glen sat on a great big boulder by the bank, one leg drawn up, and looked out across the stream. The wood came down almost to the banks of the river that side of it, this side had been cleared and brought under cultivation. It grew bananas that shot eleven hands.

The boulder he sat on was a dull slate colour. Its cast shadow on the water was the deepest blue.

The water in the pool itself was a kind of cool blue-grey, and gold and silver went in curiously woven threads across it, in uneven loops and undulations where the ripples ran.

He could see the limbs of the trees across the river moving, restless with thrust and parry in the wind. But the sound of the wind in the trees came to a hush at the edge of the river, was lost in the far thunder of the fall.

The fall itself was around another bend in the river, where it turned back again, another loop in its serpentine journeying to the sea.

Glen brought his chin down to his knee, clasped his hands about that ankle, sat still, like that, staring deep into the wood beyond.

Presently a great plumed bird, with black and red and gold markings, lighted on the branch of a spread cedar beyond the pool.

It was a strange bird, like none that had ever been seen in these parts before.

It filled the boy with wonder. "Look, Glen!" he cried. "Ever seen a bird like that in all you' life before?"

Glen shook his head and asked for silence with his finger raised half way to his lips.

The boy drew closer to him, wading slowly across the water.
He whispered hoarsely: "Gee, if I only had a gun!"

The bird flapped its wings, and lifted in the air again, and flew away, going deep into the wood.

Glen looked at George now, his gaze released from its enchantment.

"Mean to say you would kill a bird like that?"

"Good eatin' bird, it seems to me," said George.

Glen turned his head away from him in sudden disgust.

"You ought to be ashamed of you'self, you hongry?"

George was abashed, but for a moment only.

His face suddenly lit with excitement, his mind tormenting him with a new dream about growing up.

His voice became low and husky.

"Come next bird-season, you goin' let me shoot you' gun?"

"Shoot my gun, eh? Not if I know it."

"Awe Glen, don't be like that, Ah 'most man-size already. Man, you ask me, Ah'm bigger 'an some."

"I'll maybe think about it – come next bird-season."

And that was all he could wheedle out of Glen.

He hit the water a resounding whack with the flat of his hand.

"Jeez, it's hot!" he said, squeezing his hands together.

"Serves you right, you splashed water all over me," said Glen.

He said, dragging his sleeve across his face:

"What made you do it?"

George grinned, impishly: "Just felt to slap somep'n, you know that way?"

"I know somep'n I could slap right this minute!"

And George said, quickly: "Miriam!" and ducked.

With three feet of water between them he grinned again and said: "You should an' well up an' slap that gal."

Something about the way he said it, the impish look on his face, Glen started to laugh; suddenly checked it.

He got up, stretched his leg a little to ease the cramp in it. "You know what's good you get yourself dressed, come on back up to the shop," he said.

He turned and walked slowly down toward the path.

8

Amos had formed the habit of dropping in at the shop afternoons, and staying on till closing time. This afternoon when he got there, he found Jake alone, and this suited him. Glen and George had gone off to get firewood for the house. At least George had gone to get the firewood; it was one of his duties; and Glen said he would go along with him, pretending not to notice the mischievous smile it fetched to George's impish face.

Amos came into the shop, with that hunched, dragging gait, sat down on a stool, and put down his accordion on the floor beside him. Jake sat on an upturned keg over by the window, staring out through the window thoughtfully, and he had the Bible open on his knee. His thumb marked the place where he had stopped reading and, with his elbow on the windowsill, he picked his front teeth with a fingernail.

Amos said: "They caught the man who chopped-up his paramour. They found him hanging from a tree limb in the wood, and they cut him down." He stopped, as though weighing the consequences in his mind. "Guess they might just as well have made him stay on the limb where he was; be saving themselves some trouble if they had."

Jake just looked at him and didn't say anything.

"Well, they going to hang him anyway, ain't they?"

Amos laughed, but it wasn't a pleasant laugh.

"I suppose to get their proper revenge, they got to torture him a bit first."

"How you mean?"

"Well look, Jake, the poor cuss been haunted ever since he done what he done. So he gets up into a tree and tries to hang himself. Because hanging then is easier than bearing his thoughts. So what they do to him but cut him down, and throw him in a cell. He is going to languish there for months before they get around to hanging him themselves."

"That's different," said Jake, "it's the law."

"I don't believe you really feel the way you talk, Jake," Amos said.

"How?"

"Just like you saying something over they taught you way back in school, that's how."

Jake looked at him, looked away, shrugged. He kept drumming with the fingers of his hand that rested on the windowsill now.

Amos reached down, took up the accordion, played a few vagrant notes. Then he stopped playing, and said: "That she-mule of Jackson's fall him, broke his leg last week."

Jake said: "Yes, man, I heard all about it already."

"Hm! The way he used to brag about that mule!"

"You sound as though you were glad about it. You think it was a good thing, eh?"

"Why you say that, Jake? Was only commenting…"

"Yes, pardner, that's what I mean. You commenting that way. Or don't I make meself plain?"

Amos scowled at him.

"You try to make somep'n out of everything I say."

"You're always talking about people's misfortunes. Just like you get a big kick out of it. That's what I mean."

"Look, Jake, I didn't mean nothing like that. Nothing like that at all."

"Awe, you give me a pain sometimes."

That made Amos shut up immediately; and presently the silence inside the shop was something you could hit with a hammer, and it wouldn't break.

Amos reached for his accordion again, and started to play. Broke off suddenly, as before:

Jake said: "Why you stop?"

"Oh, nothing."

"Well, play man, play."

He played a mournful tune in a minor key of his own making, and Jake over by the window fell to brooding in his mind.

He tried to figure out why it was that he encouraged the ugly little hunchback about him, and could not find the answer. In a way he liked Amos, and sometimes he hated him. Perhaps it was that he liked the little man on the whole, but there were things about him he hated worse than poison.

He stole a glance at Amos, and suddenly a picture formed in his mind. It was the picture of David playing before Saul to exorcise the evil spirit that had come upon him. And his brows came together in a frown.

So that was it after all, he encouraged Amos not for Amos's sake, but because of the good that he got out of it. And then another thought came, and put this one out of his mind.

He thought the reason why he encouraged Amos about him was because he wanted to overlay the other's weakness with his own strength, as a man might put his own coat about another to shield him from the cold.

He stood up suddenly and laid the Bible aside. He walked slowly toward the door, kicking his feet against the floor a little as he went. And then he went back to the window, but stood leaning against it now.

He felt uncomfortable, thinking about himself and Amos, and he wanted to banish thought about it from his mind. He thought, if I was weak and helpless like Amos, I would need somebody strong to lean upon. And the thought filled him with resentment and bitterness, as though the thing itself menaced him, and he feared that it might come.

He resented, with all a strong, whole man's resentment, any thought of being dependent upon anyone for anything. But after a bit his thoughts retired out of the encircling chaos that had threatened to confound them, and he came to a still place of certitude, upon high ground, within his mind.

He saw clearly now that the link between Amos and himself was forged out of his own strength and the other's weakness. And he drew a deep breath into his lungs, and held it a little, and then let it go.

Amos came to the end of the piece he was playing, and he put the accordion down on the floor beside him. He started making himself a cigarette.

He stuck the ragged handmade cigarette into his mouth, struck a match, and sucked in the flame. He puffed out his cheeks, and let go a cloud of smoke. He threw the dead match away.

He said, very slowly and deliberately: "You know somep'n, Jake, life is a mess."

He said: "Any way you take it, it adds up about the same in the end."

"How do you mean?"

"Well, look at you and look at me, for instance. Only difference between us, we get it in the neck different ways."

Jake made a half-turn at the window to face him, started to laugh, but checked it, seemed to change his mind. His brows almost met in that frown again.

It was Amos who laughed now, as though he drew a deep satisfaction from the thought that moved under the surface of his mind.

"You see what I mean, Jake?" he said, slowly. "You bloody well see what I bloody mean?"

Jake said, irritably: "Stop swearing, man."

Amos looked at him.

"I'm sorry, Jake," was all he said.

But it was like a man speaking a parable, it sounded many notes together in the hearer's mind.

"What you sorry for?" said Jake, hating himself for asking the question, but perversely unable to stop himself asking, just the same.

And Amos answered him softly, "For everything."

There was a longish pause, and then Jake broke it presently:

"You know what's wrong with you, pardner?" he said.

"Plenty, I guess," said Amos.

Jake said: "Your quarrel is with life itself."

"What that mean, exactly?"

"I guess it has used you pretty badly, pardner. I suppose…"

"Well?" Amos's voice rang with a kind of challenge, his face working.

"You can't get anywhere by just hating it, pardner, that's all. Just trying to hit back at it all the time won't get you anywhere."

Jake said: "You want people to love you… don't stop me… yes, you do… and all you ever got instead was kicks, and that turned you sour."

"You can just quit being sorry for me, I ain't sorry for myself," said Amos, scowling at him.

And after he stopped speaking, his mouth still went on working, as though there was plenty more behind if only he could find the words.

He came down off the stool he was sitting on and limped across to the door. He cleared his throat and spat, and came back into the shop.

He said, changing the subject abruptly: "How is the carving coming, Jake? You promised you would show it to me sometime."

Jake's lips curled a little.

"I don't know why I ever made you that promise. I've never shown it to anyone."

"Except Miriam."

"She doesn't matter. She's just a child."

"She looks to me like a grown young woman."

"Nothing like that at all, old timer, she is like I say, just a child."

"How is it coming?" said Amos.

"The carving? Oh, it is coming along. It's – there's something…"

"Well?"

"Oh, forget it."

"All right, Jake. Anything you say."

Jake said, suddenly: "Look Amos, you ever read the story of Samson in the Bible?"

"Samson in the Bible? Yeh, I guess I heard about him once. He's the one the woman done dirt to with them Philistines, ain't it?"

"The woman – the woman – yes, there is a woman in it too." Amos looked at him closely.

"All right," he said, "forget it."

"…and they put out his eyes, and made him grind in the prison yard. That's what they done to him."

"Yes, yes."

Jake said, musingly, "He did good to pull down the temple upon them all – himself too."

"God forgive him for that – I wonder? Killing himself."

"Sure, why not? Didn't he do it for a cause?"

"I suppose so." Then he added: "He could have done it for revenge too; what you think?"

Jake said, somewhat irrelevantly: "It takes some courage in a man to kill himself."

"You think so, Jake? I don't know, every time I think about it hard, I come out of it thinking, hell no, that's a coward's way out."

"You don't know anything about it."

"Well, Jake, I guess you may be right."

"It takes a man with courage, I tell you. The kind of courage that Samson had, you know."

"Yes – yes. I guess you must be right."

9

It was close to dusk when Amos set out across the wood, taking the short cut to the village.

He came to the place where the two tracks crossed, sat down on the same stone.

Thoughts churned within him, half-remembered things, intuitions, fears.

He took his accordion in his hands and started to play a tune as it came out of his head.

He played a few passages, and they pleased him; he had to play them over again. When he played like that, sometimes images leapt abruptly to the forefront of his mind.

He thought, playing it over softly, listening to it intently:

"…me, settin' up on a cloud in glory, playin' upon a golden harp…"

And then the image faded as suddenly as it had come, and others, ugly ones, took its place.

He laid aside the accordion and looked up and down the track.

The silence that went before dusk in the wood, laid on about him, made him afraid. It was the sort of fear that a child might encounter, coming upon darkness, suddenly, alone.

He sat still as the stone under him, listening to the silence hushing in all around him.

Suddenly a bird flew out of the deeper part of the wood and lighted on a wild guava limb just before him.

Without thinking of it Amos reached out, picked up a stone, flung it at the bird, and was instantly sorry, with a kind of pang. His hand was straight; the bird fell to the ground with a broken wing.

He picked it up and came back and sat with it on the stone.

The bird made little futile jabs at him with its beak.

He felt the imminent death of this bird, suddenly poignantly, as it might have been his nearest and closest friend. He suffered with it in its pain, until hot tears formed in his eyes, and fell upon his wrist.

He bent down and picked up another stone.

He held the feebly struggling bird down with one hand, with the other he smashed its head to a pulp with one blow of the stone.

He sat there staring down at it for a long time, as though trying to puzzle out in the back of his mind what had made him do it at all.

Presently he woke, shook himself, opened his clasp knife, went and dug a little hole in the soft turf under the wild guava tree.

He put the dead bird in the hole, and pulled the dirt in over it. Then he set a stone over the grave.

It was his secret. And nobody would ever know what lay hidden under that stone.

He picked up his accordion and walked on quickly, following the track that would take him out to the parochial road near the village. And his fear walked with him always at his shoulder. And it went with the silence that shuddered through the wood.

A bent old woman came walking down the dusty road; she walked leaning upon a crooked stick. She came to the door of the blacksmith's shop, and stopped.

She lifted her stick and shook it before her. She said, in a croaking voice: "Repent!"

"It's old Mother Coby," said George, in a husky whisper.

"I know," said Jake. "I wonder what she wants."

"Don't bother your head about her, Jake," said Glen, "she's crazy. Best thing to do, leave her alone. She'll go away."

She was pouring out a flood of meaningless gibberish now; and every now and then the single intelligible word announced itself: "Repent!"

She glared at them, coming nearer, shaking her stick before her.

"You Jake," she said, "do not tempt the Lord thy God. For God is not mocked! Repent! Turn away from your evil ways, before the wrath of God fall upon you. Repent!"

"What's it, Mother Coby? What have I done displeasing to God?"

"The Lord said thou shalt not make any graven images; and that's what you been doing up there," pointing to the loft with her stick. Her thin voice quavered on: "With all the mystery and goings-on about it. God is not mocked. Repent! Repent before it is too late."

She said a lot more of the same kind and, when she came to an end, she turned and hobbled along the dusty road over the hill to the village.

George said, in a hoarse, awed whisper: "What she mean, boss?"

"Oh, she's crazy, let her alone," said Glen.

"I know," said Jake. "I wonder what put that in her head?"

"Don't pay it any mind at all."

But George was uneasy. He said: "She is a prophetess."

"Stuff and nonsense," said Jake. "Let's get on with the job."

10

That evening at supper Jake went to great pains to explain to Bess why it was he was not eating heartily, and enjoying his food as before. He told her about the cramping stomach pains he was having, and that he was not sleeping well at night.

"It's worry and anxiety," she said, promptly, nodding her head.

"Why, what do you know about it, Bess?"

"Dr. Warren told Miss Milly, the postmistress, so. Said it was worry and anxiety kept her from sleeping nights, and give her all them cramps in her belly."

She said, solemnly, sententiously: "I guess you must be worrying over something that worrying won't mend."

She kept bobbing her head up and down so that he did not know whether to be angry with her or to laugh.

He laughed.

"You think you know a lot, don't you?"

"Ah, I know plenty," she said. "I know there's people carry their worries like a load."

"Yes?"

"And it's an early death it gets them, that's a fact."

"You sound like an old witch, Bess."

"Maybe I do, to you, but them words is Bible-truth."

He said, getting up from the table:

"I think I'll turn in now. Had a hard day down at the shop."

"You aim to go see Dr. Warren in the morning? You should, you know."

"Cho! old women's tales."

"Old women's tales, nothing, it's the Bible-truth."

He felt suddenly irritable with her, he didn't know why.

He felt like shouting at her: "Shut up! What the hell do you know!"

But he held himself in, and walked quietly from the room instead.

Inside his bedroom he undressed slowly, sat on the side of the bed, and stared around the familiar room.

The washstand, the dressing-table, the bookcase, the shotgun on the bracket he had made for it over against the wall. And then his gaze went through the window, and slowly, imperceptibly almost, the cramping stomach pains came on.

He sat like that for a long time, trying not to think about it, until his face was bathed in sweat. He dug his hands into his sides, and retched, but nothing came.

Once he managed to belch, and he got some temporary relief, but bit by bit the pains came on again. And it was all he could do to sit still, and hold on to the bed-rail, and not groan aloud.

Dr. Warren says... what was she trying to tell him any at all? So he depended upon his very life and health on the woman who had left him for her lover... was that it?... could he accept that?

Worry and anxiety! What the hell did she know!

The pains in his stomach drew him into knots, and the sweat broke out afresh, until he felt clammy and cold.

He would just ask her for some hot water... a cup of hot water, yes... he would put some peppermint drops in it and some bicarbonate of soda and drink it down, hot. That sometimes stopped it.

Then he would bathe his face and head with bay rum, and try to sleep.

Just in case he should start her all over again on the subject of Dr. Warren, he would just go to the kitchen and get that water himself. If she said another word to him tonight, he would shout at her, he knew.

Luckily she was talking to Miriam out in the yard by the woodshed when he got to the kitchen.

He just got himself a cup of hot water, and went quietly back to his room.

11

Glen came across the yard from the woodshed, carrying an armful of split firewood, going toward the kitchen.

He had to brush past Miriam at the kitchen door.

He said, stiffly: "Excuse me."

And she giggled a little and said, "It's all right."

He dropped the firewood in the bin, and turned and looked at her.

The sight of her standing there teased him. Whether he wanted most to kiss her or to beat her, he didn't know.

"Why you stand there looking like that?" she said.

"Does it trouble you, the way I look?"

"You don't have to be rude."

"Who's being rude, I'd like to know. Isn't it you standing there asking me questions that no woman should ask?"

She flared: "What question did I ask you that's improper, I'd like to know?"

"You said, why was I looking at you. Didn't you say that, eh?"

"Sure I did, and what harm in that? Is that an improper question for a girl to ask?"

"I didn't say improper. Was you said that. All I said, you shouldn't ask."

She said, bringing her hand to her cheek. "It look like you out to pick an argument every time we meet. I don't understand you at all."

And just then, before he could answer that accusation, Bess came in from the living-room, and saw them standing there with that tension between them.

She cleared her throat.

Glen turned and saw her. He said, shortly: "Brought some firewood from the shed for you. It's in the bin when you want it."

He just gave a little twitch to his shoulders, and went outside.

Bess stood for a moment looking at Miriam's face. She said, her mouth tightening a little. "Is there something between him and you?"

But Miriam wasn't in a mood to answer what she felt were unnecessary questions tonight.

She said, pertly: "What you mean?"

"You stand there ask me what I mean, I fire you box on you' headside. Answer me this minute, you hear?"

"No."

"What you mean, no?"

"You asked me a question, Ma, I told you no. That's all."

"Hm! It had better be no. It had been anything else I'd have had something to say."

"What do you mean, Ma? Can't I have a friend?"

"Not if he means something to you, that way, you can't."

She wanted to ask, which way, but thought better of it. She said, instead: "I'm nineteen gone. You were married when you were my age."

And Bess thought that was too much, so she took her a walk over to the woodshed to give her a "good talking-to", just in case she should have occasion to raise her voice in the house, and Jake should hear.

12

Miriam had fully made up her mind that the next time she had an opportunity of speaking to Jake alone she would set her problem before him. Her opportunity came the very next night, because after supper he suddenly felt compelled to do some more work on his Samson.

She said now, as she held the lantern for him: "If a girl should be in love with a young man…" and suddenly broke off.

She felt intuitively that this was no time to talk to Jake, about this or any other matter.

There was that intense concentration in every muscle and nerve of his being. It seemed to have a hard, brittle quality about it, as though almost any moment now something might crack.

She felt it so strongly that it unnerved her a bit. The lantern wobbled in her hand.

"Hold steady," he said, breathing with his mouth.

He said, working with those steady, bold chisel strokes: "It's coming… my God, it's almost… there!"

He was speaking and breathing through his mouth all the time, so that the words came from him with a kind of hiss.

He laid down the tool he was using, and took up another one, feeling for it blindly on the bench beside him with his right hand.

She moved the lantern ever so slightly so that he might not scorch his arm against the hot shade.

The most important thing left to him in life now was his carving, and something was happening to that. He could feel it slipping away from him in some intangible manner. It was as though his hand had lost its cunning, and faltered when his mind would push ahead.

The heaviness was in his hand... in his hand...

And then another time it would be strangely the other way about... then it was a wanting of vision, a blindness, a blur...

Sometimes he could see it growing into the likeness of the vision he had of it in his mind. And then again it seemed as though it was slipping away from him, and he had lost control.

Tonight it was like that. One moment it was there; the next, it was gone.

His hand trembled, faltered, stopped... except for the trembling.

She thought, with sudden panic, oh God, he has done something wrong. Was it because her hand shook, holding the lantern?

She looked up into his face... saw him shake his head... shut his eyes tight... suddenly open them wide, like a man straining to see in the dark.

He passed his hand before his eyes now... there had been a sudden blur... he couldn't see... he passed his hand before his eyes, and cried out like a man in pain.

She shrank away, frightened, the knuckles of her other hand came up hard against her teeth.

He took his hand from his eyes, and his vision cleared. He had been at it too closely for too long, that was all. His vision cleared. He saw what perhaps nobody else looking at it could see, the coming into being of something, the image of which was locked within his mind.

His sudden, quick smile heartened her. She breathed again, was conscious of breathing.

He said, in a hushed kind of whisper, "Look at it."

And she looked, and tried to see what he saw, but her lack of vision made it impossible for her. She felt it poignantly, as though she had failed him in some important issue that involved his very life.

He said, gazing steadily at the carving, "All mine!" like that.

Her eyes questioned his face, trying to read what lay behind it, but failed in that as well. *All mine...* now what did he mean by that?

And she discovered her lips putting the thought into words, as though they went without the consent of her will.

"What you mean?"

He said, without removing his gaze from the carving. "All mine. Nothing else."

The very intensity of his gaze gave his eyes a crazy look. She was scared.

She felt she must do something to break that horrible brittle tension, or else something would crack.

She said, scarcely knowing what she was saying, just speaking the first words to her mind:

"If a girl should be in love..."

"Eh?" he said. "Love? Ha! Look at *him*!"

Her hand holding the lantern trembled violently.

"Ask him," he said. "Ask him what does *he* think of love."

He said: "It's all there, I've set it down. Or don't you see it, eh?"

Her hand was trembling violently. She couldn't find her voice. When at last it came, it was almost like a scream.

"Jake!" she said. "Jake!"

She bit down on her knuckles hard.

"Eh? Eh? What is it?"

And it was Jake's voice as she knew it that was talking to her now.

But she was too full with all kinds of mixed-up emotions to say anything. She set the lantern down on the floor, brought both hands up to her face, her shoulders shaking with her sobs.

He went and stood beside her, his arm about her shoulders, said gently: "What's the matter, eh? You not frightened? Come let us go down, then. You're tired, that's what it is."

13

George quit working the bellows when Jake lifted the red-hot lump of metal out of the furnace with the huge iron tongs and set it down on the anvil. George nipped around and took the tongs from Jake, holding the piece of molten metal steady on the anvil, and Jake and Glen took hammers and beat rhythmic strokes on it until it took the required shape under their blows.

All the while Amos sat on his stool a little apart, and looked on broodingly.

No word was spoken until the last hammer stroke fell, and Jake held up his hand to signify that it was enough. He took the tongs from George again, hefted the heavy lump of iron with it clear off the anvil, and plunged it, hissing and smoking, into an iron drum of water standing by.

George pushed his hands in his pockets, and whistled absently between his teeth.

Jake turned away from the drum and started taking off his thick leather apron.

"It must be past six o'clock,' he said. "Think we'll just call it a day."

George put his fingers between his teeth and let out a piercing whistle now. He grinned wide and big, and his face took on its most puckish expression.

He said: "That was the whistle you heard."

"Yes," said Glen, "we *heard* it all right. Right in our eardrums, we did."

Jake turned to George.

"You run along home now, and take some firewood up to the house for Bess."

"Yes, *sir*!" said George. And he said: "Gee! I wish I liked splitting firewood the way some people do," giving Glen a look, and getting set to make a dash for the door.

But Glen only said, "Get yourself a girl first."

"Girls!" said George.

Glen laughed: "You're getting a big boy now. Soon you'll be filling out those old pants so nobody'll ever know they weren't made for you."

"Still an' all, gals don't interest me," said George.

Glen said: "Boy, you got plenty to learn yet. Wait until you done fill out those pants."

He laughed, and George said, with spirit: "You gimme a

shotgun an' let's go out into the woods after birds, I'll show you!"

"All right, son," said Jake, "you run along home now, and be sure take that wood home for Bess."

"I'm not too young to have me a gal, if I wanted one," said George, giving a hitch to his pants. "I know plenty of chaps not half as big as me..."

"All right, all right. Quit braggin', now."

"I seen them without their clothes on down in the river. Laughing and jumping in the water all over. Rompin'. I seen them plenty times."

"You hide and peep at girls bathing! You ought to be ashamed of yourself."

"I wasn't peepin'. I just come upon them like that, an' then I went away."

Glen laughed: "Awe, never mind," he said, "you're a good kid."

"Gimme a shotgun an' let's go out into the woods after birds, I'd show you something!"

He walked away with his hands in his pockets, whistling a rowdy tune.

Glen said, going into the shop and hanging up his leather apron on the hook beside Jake's: "We ought to be able to deliver that job by Thursday, after all," jerking his chin at it.

"Yes," said Jake.

And after a little Glen said: "You don't need me for anything around, do you?"

"No. I guess not. You go look for your girl."

Glen just gave him a quick look. Nodded.

"Okay."

Jake said, as though he was talking to himself, speaking his thoughts aloud: "We carry on here. Nothing gets in the way."

And Glen said: "Sure. You should put that up on the board outside." He said over to himself: "*We carry on here...*"

"No need for that," said Jake. "They know it. Already we got our hands so full, soon we won't know what to do to turn around. This evening there's a rush job from the sugar estate fifteen miles away."

"And they have their own works."

"But more than they can handle. The world knows we're good. Nothing to worry about there."

"That's right. Well, so-long, Jake."

Jake made a gesture with his hand. He sat down on the bench facing Amos as Glen went out.

14

George came out of the woodshed swinging a machete in his hand. He was still whistling the same tune as he walked across the common, going to the wood beyond.

He walked a little way into the wood, and came to where an old dry tree lay on its side with little creeping withes starting to grow over it. This tree had been blown down during the hurricane last year, but when Glen came looking for firewood he didn't stop at this tree. It was being held in reserve for an emergency, like when it rained torrents, and held on like that for days, and you just couldn't get deep into the wood. So Glen didn't chop the old dry tree, and George knew why. But he just gave a glance at it now, and went over and sat down on the fallen trunk.

His hand went inside his shirt front and he took out his *guzung-fet* and looked at it. This *guzung-fet* was a kind of charm, and he had got it off a boy called Hamby.

It was a flat, almost round, dark, mottled stone, with many curious hieroglyphics scratched on its surface, and it hung about his neck in a brown, shrivelled, parchment-like bag, made from the bladder of a sheep.

Hamby had stolen the *guzung-fet* from his grandmother, and he had got it off Hamby this way.

There was a certain trick with three cards that he knew. Spotting the Joker it was called. He had won pennies off Hamby many times with this trick, and Hamby wanted to learn it for himself.

"Bwoy," said George, "if I learn you this trick it goin' cost you plenty."

"How much?" said Hamby.

George fell to thinking, and presently he said: "A man know this trick, he can never be broke. He can make money off it any time. A man could make himself rich so he wouldn't have to work, knowing a trick like this, if he just used his head, and travelled around."

Hamby agreed with all that, and said again how much did he want for learning him the trick, and George looked at him steady in the eyes and said, "I will learn you this trick for your *guzung-fet*."

At first Hamby held back, but George knew he had him along from the first. He wouldn't budge. And presently Hamby agreed.

George showed him how to work the three-card trick that he had learned off a man who had broken jail and was hiding in that wood, and George had discovered his hideout, and they became friends, and George brought him food secretly every day. He swore he would never tell, and he didn't. But the police from the next town came and surrounded the place, and took him in one day.

When George showed Hamby the three-card trick now, Hamby thought it was a cinch, and that he could work it right away. But George told him it would take him a lot of practice to get it right, and Hamby tried it again and again, and presently George left him, carrying off the *guzung-fet*, and Hamby just watched him walking away, whistling spryly, and wondered if perhaps he hadn't made a bad deal.

George took the *guzung-fet* from his shirt-front now, and looked at it long and reverently, for it was a charm that was supposed to do many wonderful things for its owner, and at first he was a little fearful of it; but now he kissed it reverently, and put it back inside his shirt-front, next to his skin, again.

Then he got up and started chopping the old dead tree. And the sound of his shrill whistling went skirling through the wood.

15

There were times when Jake, too, used to take long walks by himself into the woods, and he knew what it was that Amos got from that feeling of being withdrawn from the world. He got the same feeling from being alone with his carving. Healing went with it, and a sense of stillness and peace. And a feeling too that a man is alone in the world, and sufficient, and not dependent upon anyone. That was the feeling he got from those long walks alone, deep into the wood... and when he was alone in the loft with Samson.

Amos came to the end of the tune he was playing, and laid the accordion on the floor beside him. He cleared his throat.

"Well," he said. "You want to talk, or not?"

And Jake said, wearily: "Not particular. Got anything on your mind?"

"Just want to know, that's all," said Amos.

Jake nodded his head.

"You talk."

Suddenly Amos ceased scowling, and fingered his accordion eagerly.

"Perhaps – perhaps you would rather hear a little music, eh?"

The way he said it, the sudden eagerness in his face, made Jake laugh; and Amos was pleased. He thought, it took so little to make Amos happy.

He said: "You're all right, Amos. You're a damned decent little chap."

Amos scowled again.

"Little chap! Well, I suppose you could call me that."

"No offence, pardner. Why you so touchy?" said Jake.

"Touchy? Me? Why, I just said you could call me that, Jake." He paused. Presently: "Somehow it's all right when *you* say it."

"Forget it," said Jake.

Then presently he laughed again.

"We are a couple of queer ones, eh pardner? You and me. I guess that's why we get along together. To most people you're poison, but to me..." He laughed again, his lips curling a little: "It's just like we're kin."

And Amos said, eagerly: "You think so, Jake? Really?"

"Sure. Don't you? Look Amos, I'd like to ask you something. Why do you come here at all? I know you don't like people. You like being off some place by yourself. You've run away from people all your life. What's the difference between me and – and everybody else, that you come and sit here afternoon upon afternoon? Tell me, eh?"

Amos said, gruffly: "You just said it yourself."

"And yet I treat you like dirt – when I'm in my black moods…" He broke off. Then: "Why don't you play something?"

"You want to talk, that's why."

"What is talk? Play."

But Amos didn't play. Of a sudden he had become very thoughtful.

He said, slowly: "Just a couple of God's creatures, born out in the cold. You an' me. Kin. That's us.

"Don't know much about us being born that way, pardner. Maybe we did that ourselves."

Amos spat contemplatively on the floor, then immediately erased it with his boot.

He said: "Maybe. After all what does it matter, Jake?"

He said: "We got something in common, ain't we? You think so?"

"You grew up all crooked like that," said Jake, staring at the floor just in front of him. "You grew that way from a boy. Maybe there is that difference. Some folk say your mind is twisted, the same. And sometimes I believe them."

But Amos only laughed.

He said: "Still an' all, we mix."

Jake got up suddenly, with a gesture of impatience. "For Christ sake," he said, "let's talk about something else."

And Amos looked at him humbly, almost imploringly.

"What you want to talk about now, Jake?"

"How should I know? Anything but about ourselves. Christ, man, just talk!"

Amos shook his head.

"You're still worrying about that woman. I know."

Jake swung on him savagely: "Don't be a fool!"

"Still an' all…"

But Jake, his gorge rising, shouted at him: "Don't be a dope, Amos. Quit talking about *her*, you hear?"

An awkward silence fell between them. Amos looked down at

his boots, he scuffed at some metal shavings on the ground with one of them.

Presently he said: "Pansy Thomas – the butcher's girl you know her, Jake. She's going to have a baby. They say – guess who they say the father is." He laughed coarsely. "I'd give you from now till midnight, an' you wouldn't guess. They say the father is – "

"Shut your face!" Jake swung on him angrily. "I don't want to hear none of your filthy gossip tonight." He turned away to the window. "What do I care about little Pansy Thomas and her trouble, anyway... or any of them... and what do you care? Do you care anything? Answer me. Hell, no!"

Amos shook his head, and echoed after him: "No."

"Well then, why you wallow in it up to the neck, like that?"

"I don't," he said, quickly. And then: "I don't know, Jake."

And they were silent for a spell after that.

Presently Jake turned from staring out of the window.

"I guess it just makes you feel that you're getting even with the world – that must be it."

And Amos said, shamefaced: "I – I never thought about it."

Jake swung away from the window, kicked a lump of coal from under his feet.

"I am sorry, pardner," he said. "I didn't mean to bawl you out like that – forget it."

"I don't mind..." Amos began.

And Jake said again: "Awe, forget it."

16

Miriam in the kitchen peeling yams caught herself out thinking those thoughts again... about Glen and herself, his wanting her to meet him clandestinely like that, and what she should do about it.

She shook her head, and with an effort of will put the thought out of her mind.

She went on peeling the yams... and like one nodding himself to sleep, with the encroachment of weariness over a tiresome chore, she caught herself at it again...

If a girl should be in love…

She shook her head, blinked her eyes wide open, stared a little, out in front of her, at the bare whitewashed wall, and started to sing.

That was better. Singing like that she could keep her thoughts under control.

She sang:

"*Brown-skin gal, stay home an' mind baby…*" thrusting those nagging thoughts behind her.

She stared at the blank wall in front of her, singing, her hands automatically performing the domestic chore of peeling the yams, and slipping them into the iron pot in front of her.

And then the knife just slipped, she couldn't say how, and she cut her finger.

It was a nasty cut, and she looked at it an instant, holding it up before her face, frightened.

The blood ran down her hand and wrist, and fell on her dress.

She was sitting like that, scared, confused, not knowing what to do, when Glen came in through the door.

He just looked at her. Saw the blood. A little indrawn hissing sound came from his lips as he started across to her.

He said, standing hesitant before her: "You cut yourself bad."

And she said: "Yes," holding the cut finger up for him to look at it, and started to laugh.

She was sitting on an upturned box, and she laughed so much, rocking about back and forth on the box, it nearly fell over with her. It would have, too, only Glen had the presence of mind to bend down, grab her with both arms, drag her to her feet, and he stood there for a while just holding her against him like that.

It seemed now all his presence of mind deserted him, and he just stood holding her hand against him like that, as though he couldn't think what next to do.

She stopped laughing suddenly, and said, with her lips against his ear:

"You – you think you could tie it up for me?"

That brought him back to the immediacy of the situation.

"Yes," he said, "oh yes," his arms relaxing a bit. "Let me see it no', honey; it hurt you much?"

"Not – not too much."

She started to get the giggles again.

And he said, seriously, looking at her: "I'll have to find some way to make you stop, if you keep on doing that."

She stopped giggling. And he got mercurochrome and a roll of adhesive tape from the first-aid kit in the cabinet behind the door, dressed and bound up the cut finger. Then he made her sit down on the box again, and he sat down beside her, and they started to talk.

But the talk didn't get beyond the most trivial and commonplace things. Not once did they speak about the thing that was in the forefront of their minds.

Presently Miriam held up a hand to silence him. She said, "Hark!"

They could hear Bess singing throatily to herself back in the house.

17

Amos started playing a few tentative notes on the accordion. He felt as a dog feels after he has just been whipped for something. He wanted to rehabilitate himself in Jake's esteem again.

And Jake said, sitting down, clasping his hands about his knees: "That's right, Amos. Let her go. Play."

"What you have a fancy for?"

"Anything, just let her rip."

But before Amos could get properly started there was an interruption. Two elderly men came into the blacksmith's shop. They were Massa Butty and Tata Joe, two old cronies, and a couple of busybodies on top of that. They came in now and sat down without waiting to be asked. And Jake said, grinning at them, "Take a seat, Massa Butty, take a seat, Tata Joe."

And the two old cronies looked at each other and shook their heads and laughed.

They said, together: "Jake! He's a one for his joke!" as though they had rehearsed it.

The moment the two old men came in, Amos got up and slunk out of the shop, and nobody even noticed when he went.

"Well, Jake?" said Massa Butty, resting his hands on his knees, and leaning forward a bit. "How goes it?"

And Tata Joe said: "How goes?"

Jake grunted noncommittally.

"Just dropped in to say 'howdy'," said Massa Butty.

"Passin' by, you know," said Tata Joe.

Massa Butty said again: "How's things Jake?"

And Jake said: "Fine. Like I said before."

Tata Joe laughed, shook his head: "This Jake!"

Massa Butty laughed too. Suddenly stopped laughing, looked about the shop. "Hm! What happened to your friend? He was here when we come in."

"Guess he must have gone out again. Don't mind him. He isn't used to company."

The two old men laughed, as though he had given them a joke. They slapped their thighs, and rocked back and forth, laughing.

"This Jake!" they said together, rubbing their eyes. "Must have his little joke."

Then Massa Butty became serious all of a sudden.

He said: "Jake, we been thinking..."

"Yes, Jake, we been thinking," said Tata Joe.

"What! The two of you together? Don't tell me!"

"Yes Jake, we been puttin' our old heads together," said Massa Butty.

"Massa Butty here, an' me; the two of us together," said Tata Joe.

"All right," said Jake. "So what?"

Massa Butty leaned forward slightly, fixed him with his gaze.

"You think it's right you should be doing this?" he said.

"Why not?" said Jake. "What's wrong with me now? What's wrong with what I'm doing? I'm minding my own business, I'm not harming anyone."

"*Tsk! Tsk!* Don't take it like that, Jake," said Tata Joe. "We're your friends."

"Friends of your father before you, we were."

"That's right. We was friends of your pa before you was born."

Jake said, patiently: "I know."

"You're fit for better things, Jake," said Tata Joe.

"Like what, for instance?" said Jake.

"Things that take your kind of education," said Massa Butty. "You mean to be a blacksmith all your life?"

"What's wrong with being a blacksmith?" said Jake.

"And with your education, the learnin' you've got," said Tata Joe, scratching his old head. "You'd just be throwing yourself away."

"You're not happy here, Jake. I know it. And the reason is you should be doing something else. Bigger things. You could be a Public Works foreman as easy as *that*!"

Massa Butty snapped his fingers in the air before him.

"Yes, man," said Tata Joe, nodding his head, "with the learnin' you've got."

"They're building a new road through Burnt Hill right now…"

"Or even a school teacher. I wouldn't put it past you."

"Why don't you go away, Jake?" said Massa Butty, suddenly, out of a little silence, in which they just sat and shook their heads.

Jake got up quickly: "So that's it, eh!"

"Now don't get us wrong, Jake," said Massa Butty. "It's not that we aren't proud to have you in the district, eh, Tata Joe?"

"Not anything like that at all, Massa Butty."

Jake took two steps inside the shop a bit, and two steps back again. He struck the palm of his hand with his fist. He said:

"I'm much obliged to you, friends. But let me try and show you something. If there was no one to carry on this trade, what would happen to all the people around who need a blacksmith to mend or make things for them? Tell me that."

He smiled at them with great tolerance, looking from one to the other. Then, because they had no answer for him, he went on.

"From the day I fixed old Mother Bado's bedspring for her," a little smile of reminiscence twitched the corners of his lips, "her pains left her, and she has never been bothered with them since. You think that's nothing? I done more for that old woman than all the doctors she ever been to done for her. And she's never forgotten it, either. Every time she passes this way she stops and has a chat – God bless her."

He looked from one to the other; they were not looking at him. The little smile deepened at the corners of his lips.

"People say, and rightly too, even though it may sound like boasting, that Jake the blacksmith, that's me, can make or mend most anything – from a pin to an anchor, from a bedspring to a tombstone, from a hasp-and-staple to a sewing machine."

The two men nodded their heads in silent agreement, and after a bit Jake went on:

"I might have found other things to do that I liked better, that would bring in more money, perhaps; but nothing that would have served the needs of a greater number of people. My father owned this shop before me. He didn't think himself too good to be a blacksmith. He gave me opportunities he never had. But that doesn't mean he fixed it so I'd be too good to work, as he did, at this trade. It suits me."

There was silence in the shop when he had finished speaking. Presently Massa Butty started speaking, but tentatively, as though he was not quite sure of his ground:

"I know there's other things you're interested in," he said, jerking his head in the direction of the loft behind him. "All that goes on back there... with all the mystery about it. I'm not trying to say it isn't a fine thing for a man to be able to do them things, but what's it get you? That's what I'd like to know."

Jake laughed: "Don't let it worry you," he said, rising as though to signify that the interview was over. "Anyway it was mighty good of you two old friends of my father's to drop in on me like this. How's my goddaughter Esmeralda, Tata Joe?"

"She's doin' fine, Jake," said Tata Joe. "She sends howdy for you."

"That reminds me, I got something for her. Won't be a minute."

He went back into the room.

The two men stood in the entrance of the shop. They looked at each other, shook their heads. Jake had gone into a little room just behind the shop.

"He's been a different man, Tata Joe, ever since the woman run away," said Massa Butty.

"Beats me how he stands that muggin, Amos, around him all the time, like that," said Tata Joe.

"For all that I say he's better rid of her – the little fly-by-night bitch!" said Massa Butty, venomously, and spat out the door. "Always held them yaller-skin lowland gals never brought no good with them. They're bad luck, that's what."

"And as the saying goes, that's worse than obeah. I wonder what he's got in there for Esmeralda?"

"Sure to be something that ain't a sight of good to anyone."

"*S-s-sh!* He's coming."

Jake came over to them, carrying a small object in his hands. It was a little carving in ebony. He put it into Tata Joe's hands.

"Be Jesus!" said Massa Butty, taking one look at it. "It's a little dawl-baby! Ain't it cute, Tata Joe?"

"Just the thing Esmeralda would like to get from her god-pappy. Eh, Massa Butty?" said Tata Joe.

The two men giggled their appreciation of the "dawl-baby", and passed it from one to the other.

"You chipped that out yourself, I bet," said Massa Butty.

And Jake laughed and said: "I chipped it out myself, yes, like you say. Give it to Esmeralda with my best love, Tata Joe."

"You couldn't have given her a better thing," said Tata Joe.

All the while he was talking Jake was gently, unostentatiously, ushering them out through the door; almost without their noticing it they were outside, murmuring their farewells.

"So-long, Jake. Keep hearty," they said together, the way people with little vocabulary, who have lived long in each other's pockets, do on occasions.

"So-long. Walk good!' said Jake.

18

Bess was singing to herself in a husky, throaty voice as she worked. She had a long-handled broom in her hands. She was sweeping cobwebs off the ceiling. She hated spiders, and was also afraid of them. Perhaps she hated them so because she was afraid of them. They were one of the crosses she had to bear in life. They wouldn't leave her alone. She would cobweb a room, and turn her back, and the spiders would invade it again.

She was always careful not to kill one of them. It was bad luck to kill a spider. Spider was Bra' Annancy. Smart fellow. Too smart. Cunning... Bra' Annancy. She was scared of them.

You killed one of them spiders, and then you start dropping things out of your hands. Things just dropped from you and broke, and it was on account of the spider you had killed. Was Bra' Annancy's revenge on you for killing one of his family.

So she wasn't taking any chances with any of Bra' Annancy's breed. She took great pains sweeping the cobwebs off the ceiling, and when a spider got tangled in his own web, or got himself stuck to the end of the broom, she put the broom through the window and shook him off outside.

Of course he would come back in again, soon's she had turned her back, but she wasn't taking any chances, no sir!

Goodness gracious! it was past time for her to start putting the supper on the table... seeing she had got so far already, she'd just finish this room.

Without her noticing it a spider spun a long thin web from where it had lodged on the broom. The next swing she took with it the spider swung out from her, and in again. It landed softly on the side of her cheek, started immediately to crawl around to the back of her neck.

She screamed... without thinking what she was doing, slapped at it. The spider was squashed to a greyish sticky pulp under her heavy hand.

The broom swung, this time without her will or direction. It swept a vase off the dressing table, shattered it to splinters on the floor. She screamed again, jumped, tripped over the broom stick, sat down with a thud that went jarring clear through her plump body.

When Miriam and Glen came running from the kitchen they found her sitting there.

"What's the matter, Ma?" said Miriam.

Glen went over to her, put his hands under her armpits, from behind, started to make a great big heave to get her to her feet.

"Wait," she said. "Tek time."

"Try to help yourself up," said Glen, taking a big breath.

Miriam stood rocking a little at the door, with her hand over her mouth.

"Come again," said Glen, and he gave another heave.

Bess was breathing hard.

"Wait,' she said. "I feel as though I have broken something… please God is only me corset… but do tek time!"

19

Amos came back into the shop almost as soon as the two old cronies had left. He just slunk in, the way he had gone.

Jake sat on the bench, his hands clasped behind his head, leaned back against the wall.

Amos sat on the stool, rolled himself a cigarette, smoked in silence.

They sat like that for a long time.

Occasionally one or other of them started to talk, but in a desultory fashion, without zest.

It was the time of early rising of the moon.

Outside the sky was blackening quickly, as though making ready for one of those sudden thunderstorms.

Dusk thickened quickly, and the moon rose between the forked branches of a stark cinnamon tree.

Amos said: "Saw them going down the road talking and shaking their heads. What they want anyway?"

And Jake said, in a faraway voice: "The moon is coming up… so soon!" And after a bit he said: "Don't bother your head about them, let 'em be."

It got darker and darker quickly.

And Amos said, presently, "It's past supper time."

But Jake seemed not to hear him.

He said, after a silence of seconds: "I could sit here all night and look at the moon."

Lightning flickered in the distance, and thunder rolled.

"Storm coming up," said Jake.

The eeriness, and the silence, and the thought of lightning coming nearer every minute, unnerved Amos. He hated lightning, in truth he was scared of it, but he kept it a secret, ashamed to let anyone know.

He got off the stool.

"It's getting dark," he said. "Shall I light the lantern?"

Jake said: "We're going to have rain. I can feel it inside me."

"Yes," said Amos.

And almost simultaneously there was a great double flash of lightning, followed by a loud clap of thunder that made him jump.

Jake laughed softly inside his throat, as though at something funny.

"Ever heard of lightning without thunder?"

"Lightning without thunder... what you mean?"

"I mean you never see that kind of forked-lightning, without thunder coming after," said Jake.

And Amos said: "M-m-m!"

Lightning shook a blade across the sky again, the darkness recoiled before it, and then it went out. And when the thunder came, at length, Jake's laughter rolled with it.

"Almost thought it would never come that time... or perhaps it would bring with it the end of the world... the world underneath us, holding us up... going out like a spark in darkness... like one of them shooting stars in the sky."

He laughed again, and said: "Why not?"

Amos moved about restlessly. He was scared of the lightning, but he didn't want Jake to know it.

He said, irritably: "What's getting you, Jake?"

"I say you never see that kind of lightning without thunder," said Jake, sitting up suddenly. "And do you know what that would mean if that should happen? It would mean the lightning had struck you, cold... blotted you out." He made a gesture with his hand. "It would mean its bolt had entered into you... and you were lying there dead and cold."

Amos swung on him, almost screamed in a high-pitched voice: "Stop it, Jake. For Christ sake!"

But Jake went on as though he hadn't heard him.

"And it wouldn't make any difference to you how much the thunder rolled on overhead... you wouldn't be able to hear it, that's all. You'd be good an' dead."

Amos's voice cracked a little at the edge: "You going crazy?" he said.

And Jake's voice was calm now, and distant.

"No. I'm thinking my thoughts out aloud, that's all."

And then he said, a little contemptuously: "What's the matter; you scared?"

"Scared? Me? Course I'm not!" said Amos.

He went back and sat on the stool.

A sudden rattle of big rain fell, hitting the tin roof like pebbles tossed in the air. And after that, silence. And darkness hung about them, thick as a curtain; you could almost feel it, it was moist and warm.

"Light the lantern,' said Jake. "We'll take a look at him now, eh? What you say to that?"

"Anything you say, Jake. It's okay by me."

Almost as soon as he got the lantern going, the moon broke from behind a dark cloud.

"He ought to look good with the moonlight coming in full on him through the window," said Jake.

Amos stood silent, holding the lantern, waiting for Jake to go first.

"You go before," said Jake.

They climbed the ladder to the loft that way.

They came to a halt on the threshold. Amos could hear Jake's breathing just over his shoulder.

"Take a look at Samson now. You haven't had a sight of him yet, and I know you're just dying with curiosity. Go on now, get closer up to him. Hold the lantern high, so you can see."

Amos, holding the lantern high, approached the carving fearfully, and his hand was trembling, he didn't know why.

Jake remained standing a few paces behind him, and his voice went on in that same low, distant monotone:

"You see? They have put out his eyes out of his head. The Philistines done that to him. Because he was a strong man, and they were afraid. Go on, get right up close. What you scared about? There's nothing going to harm you... And now he is leaning forward a little, bent with the great burden he has to bear; and his hand is resting on the shoulder of a little lad. Samson, leaning on a little lad! For you see, now he is weak, and wanting. Because they have put out his eyes."

He stopped, groping for words, and he went on again, in the same voice as before:

"Look, Amos, if you could gather up all the suffering there is in the world... of all the folks who had lost their way in some kind of darkness, and of all who have known any kind of lack that human flesh and spirit can know... take all that suffering, and add it up... you would get something like that – that hopeless, uneven slump of the shoulders, that face. Eh?"

"Yes. And add to that, all the suffering of all the bent and twisted bodies that make men turn away from them – that too, I guess. And what it means to go on living inside one of them maimed and twisted bodies, cursing your parents for being born."

But Jake went on as though he hadn't heard him, and it might be he only imagined he had spoken aloud but the words hadn't left his lips at all.

"But to what end, Amos? Where does the finger point? Down what blind road... through what blank wall... to what? Where will he take that burden to its last resting-place, and set it down? And be restored to himself again, whole? That's what it is, Amos. That's what it calls for, you understand? And it will not come. Something else, but not that."

Amos stammered: "I – I can't figure it out either, Jake."

"And still it is somewhere. You must believe that. Else what do you believe?"

Outside lightning whipped across the sky, thunder rolled and drummed through the valley. It was lost in the distance, and then seemed to turn, like an angry bull, and roll back up the valley again.

There was a little window high in the loft and, when the lightning licked outside, the window lit all over it instantly, and the light reached to the four corners of the room. Amos was shaking, so that the lantern nearly fell from his hand. He suddenly turned and made a blind rush for the ladder. But Jake put an arm out and stopped him, held him pinned to his side, struggling with all his strength, with one hand.

"Let me go, Jake. Let me get out of here."

"Keep still, can't you?"

"All right,' panting, "I promise… but let me go."

Jake released him, and went on talking, as though there had been no interruption.

"But where, Amos, where? Do you want me to tell you? It is here!' Striking his forehead with the heel of his hand. "Here inside my head… inside my brain… inside my breast, maybe… but here, somewhere." He stopped, but his lips were still working, and then the words started to come again: "But since I cannot find it, it is nowhere, and that's crazy. Everything is crazy. You are crazy, Amos, and so am I."

And Amos said, taking a single step toward him: "Jake!"

"My hands have gone back on me." He held them up before him, close to his face. "I cannot make it come."

He took two strides and stood immediately in front of the statue. And then he said in a low, tense voice: "Come here, Amos."

Amos came and stood beside him.

"Look… you see what I see?"

Amos looked, and he tried to say something, but words would not come to him.

"Do you see what I see?" said Jake. And without taking his eyes off the statue: "Why don't you say something? Are you dumb?" His hand reached out, and clutched the other's shoulder. "You are shaking like a leaf! Are you afraid? There's nothing here to be afraid of. There's nobody going to hurt you."

Amos stammered: "It – it beats me how you do it, Jake – beats me how – how it all comes to you, like…"

"Don't stall. You said all that over already. Come; out with it; straight."

And Amos said, slowly: "I see it, Jake. What – what you wanted me to see. Yes, I see it now. I see what you mean. It ain't Samson anymore, is what you mean; ain't it?"

"What is it, then?" tensely. "Tell me. Perhaps you can tell me."
"No. I can't, either. I want to get out of here."
"Wait, man. Come back here – "

But Amos was already stumbling toward the head of the ladder; going down it, anyhow, just as fast as he could.

Jake picked up the lantern and came down the ladder slowly. And the lightning seemed to make swordplay around him... a long and terrifying crash and roll of thunder... lightning again... he seemed poised there, waiting an anxious interval... nothing...

And presently Amos came stumbling blindly into the shop again, hearing the crash of the lantern as it fell, and the thud that went with it... saw, in the sudden play of lightning about it, what huddled there... went down on his knees beside it, trying to shake him awake... his fear rising in him, choking him, sound tearing free from his tight throat at last, a thin, high scream: "Jake! Jake!"

THREE

There were some people in the district who held that God had sent His lightning to strike Jake and blind him for life because he was too proud.

Some of the older ones, when they talked it over in pubs, and waiting in the village stores to be served, recollected that there hadn't been a single case of lightning striking anyone in that district in over fifty years.

The last manifestation of this divine displeasure that anyone could remember was when Septimus Sylvester was struck so that he was all twisted up, and stayed that way till the day he died. But then, it was recalled, Septimus was always an infidel and a terrible man for drinking and swearing, and nobody was surprised.

It was cited against Jake, and in vindication of the Almighty, that Jake had stopped away from church going on three months, although he kept up his dues.

It was also reliably reported that when Parson Evenet had called to see him, to bring him back to grace, shortly after his woman run away, he acted strong-headed and stiff-necked, and argued with the parson about things that no man had any right to question.

Yes, there was no getting around it, Jake had set himself up against the Almighty, and now he had brought down the vengeance of God upon himself.

Old Mother Coby came down the street shaking her pimento stick that was as crooked as herself, and she spittled a little at the lips, and made curious, but convincing talk.

And a lot of people stopped and gathered around to listen to her, because she was half-crazy, and accounted to be in the secret councils of God, and to have the gift of prophecy, and of "tongues". Sometimes she gave utterance to things speaking in a strange language that nobody could understand. And then it was that the spirit was upon her, so they stood around and listened just the same.

She said now: "The Lord set it down, thou shalt not make any graven images; and that's the very thing Jake done. I warned him. And now you see what happen. He been making them images a long time, and it's all contrary to the word of God."

They nodded their assent to this, and another credit was chalked up in their consciences to God's account, in this matter concerning Himself and Jake.

"God can't be wrong; he will not be mocked by evil men," old Mother Coby shouted, shaking her stick at them. "Judgment is mine, saith the Lord. Repent!"

And somehow they went home satisfied in their minds with the knowledge that justice had been done.

2

Jake himself seemed to be strangely humbled by the fate that had overtaken him. When he was well enough, they took him from the hospital, home. He sat by himself and brooded most of the time. He seemed not to want to talk to anyone. But little by little this attitude relaxed. And now he seemed to welcome people about him.

Bess came to live in the house, and Miriam remained with her Granny at the cottage down the road. But in the days Miriam read to him often, and if she stayed away for long, he would ask for her. And she would come and sit on a stool beside him, and read aloud to him, to take his mind away from the black thoughts that gathered about him like angry thunderheads.

Little by little he learned to get around without the aid of a stick, and he always resented, even from the first, anyone's offer of assistance.

Again there were times when he was rebellious, and his black moods would make everyone afraid to come near him. All except Bess. No matter what he said or did, she never took offence, and she was not scared of him one little bit. She treated him rather like a fractious child, and after a time if anything it was Jake who was a little afraid of her. She wore him down with her nonresistance and her patience. And he could find no remedy whatever for this.

One day Miriam started to read to him from the Bible.

He put his hand out and touched her on the shoulder, shook his head.

"Not that – not today," he said.

"What would you like me to read, then?"

"The newspaper."

She brought the newspaper and started reading the headlines aloud, first, and every now and then he would stop her and say.

"Let's hear what that says."

She read aloud the caption: "THE BOY WHO HAD TO GET BANANAS".

And he said: "That sounds good, read it out."

It was the story of a little English 12-month-old boy baby suffering from a rare disease, and the only food allowed him by the doctors was bananas. Three of them per day. Due to the recent hurricane it was becoming increasingly difficult to get bananas in England. So an airways company got busy and flew a bunch of five dozen bananas to England, and that saved the boy's life.

"Well now, just fancy that," said Jake.

He seemed to be turning this over in his mind for a while, and presently he said:

"You seen Amos?"

"Eh? Amos? No, Jake," said Miriam.

And Jake was silent for a while, and she was going to ask him why did he want to know if she had seen Amos, but before she could open her mouth, he shook his head a little and said: "Well, never mind."

But the little incident disturbed her, and she went to Bess about it.

3

It seemed a curious coincidence that Amos who had stopped away for weeks dropped in the next afternoon to see Jake.

Jake was pleased to see him. In weeks he had not laughed or chatted so much. And Bess, looking on, smiling, took her apron in her hands, as though she was wiping them, smiled benevolently, shook her head over the incident as though it was the most remarkable phenomenon, and went quietly back to the kitchen, leaving them alone.

"...all the same for a time you tried to avoid me. You kept away so long I thought you didn't want ever to see me again," said Jake.

And Amos moved about the room a little uncomfortably.

"It's not anything like that, Jake," he said, sitting down on the stool now. "I thought you'd rather I didn't hang around so much, that's all."

"You really thought that, pardner?" Jake laughed.

It was a gentle, almost wistful laugh.

"And yet you are about the only link I have with – the other life. Without you, I... oh well, never mind."

"I got me a job, you know," said Amos, quickly. "Up at Walcott's store."

"Oh, good."

Amos spread his hands, made a little gesture with them, brought them down to his knees again.

"Nothing much," he said. "Just keeping the place tidy and running errands. But it was somep'n to do, and I like doing somep'n."

"Yes; of course. I understand that," said Jake.

And after a bit, he said: "Sure. Sure. It's good to have something to keep you – occupied all the time." A short, clipped laugh; then: "Gets kind of lonely down here – the evenings, especially... when there's nobody about – except Bess, that is."

"Yeh. I know."

Another lapse in the conversation, and Amos said again: "She's good to you, eh, Jake?"

"Bess? She's more than that, Amos…" He broke off. Laughed. "It – it makes me kind of humble. Ain't it curious."

"Yes," said Amos, and he looked at his hands as though he didn't know where to put them, and let them lapse against his knees again.

From outside they could hear the sound of someone chopping with an axe.

"That's Glen," said Jake. "He still comes around. He's running the shop now, you know. He's in love with Miriam. Been for a long time. I only guessed it recently. Ain't that curious, too?"

"Funny things happen," said Amos, and he couldn't think of anything else to say.

Jake went on: "She sometimes comes in and reads to me. Miriam, you know." A pause. "But a man must have someone every now and then to talk to. Someone like his own kin, you know."

"Yes," said Amos.

"Folks drop in all the time," said Jake. "There's Massa Butty, and Tata Joe. Yes, and little Esmeralda. Come to look for her god-pappy."

He laughed, quietly. And Amos laughed a little too.

"Yes. I see what you mean," said Amos.

"That's funny too. Imagine me talking to you about things like this; as though they were the most important things in life. And you sitting there saying, I see what you mean."

Amos didn't say anything.

And Jake said: "Awe hell, I just go on talking, talking…"

"Talk," said Amos. "You want to talk."

"You tell me something, man," said Jake.

Amos cleared his throat.

"All right," he said.

And then he said: "Awe hell, Jake, I don't know what to say."

"Just sit still, then," said Jake. "Man, it's good just to have you around."

"Gosh, Jake – "

"Eh?"

"Oh, nothing. Somep'n I was going to tell you. It's slipped me now."

"Don't worry. It'll come to you again. How's business, Amos?"

"Like I said before, Jake. Just so and so."

After a longish silence, Jake said: "You believe, Amos, that something a man is creating out of himself like can – can take itself a soul of its own, so to speak – with ideas of its own, that you never put there?"

"Well, I don't know Jake. Where you get them ideas, anyway?"

"Awe, let's forget it."

But after a bit he started on it again.

"And at last it takes its own end into its own hands, in a manner of speaking, and becomes what it wants to be, declaring its own form and meaning, that wasn't in the man…"

"Hm! All them big words."

"Never mind that. Think of what I'm trying to tell you. I want you should think about it real hard."

"All right, Jake."

"What you see, for instance, is a man carving a block of wood; but that's not all. You must understand that he is first of all a creator, that man, whoever he is. He's like God, brooding over that bit of wood or stone. You get that?"

"Sure, that's easy."

"Well then how does God stand, with the man he creates?"

"Eh? What you mean?"

"Does he create him down to the last atom and pulse of life and intelligence and will that's inside him? That's what I mean."

"I don't know nothing about them things, Jake."

"It seems I been sitting here thinking about nothing else for months."

"I know. And you shouldn't. What does a man want to go thinking about all those things for? What good it get him? A man starts thinking that way, he's bound to go crazy some day, that's what. You take my word for it, Jake, and leave all them things alone."

"Oh, what's the difference? What you think about yourself, Amos? Did you at some time take over from God, in making yourself what you are today? Or does he have the last word in everything that is formed in all of us – you, me?"

Amos got up off the stool.

"Look, Jake, I really ought to be getting along now. I got plenty to do."

"All right, if you can't stand to hear me talk…"

"It's not that at all."

"Well?"

"Well, perhaps I can stay for a bit yet."

He sat down on the stool again.

"You were telling me about a job you had, Amos, what happened to it, you quit?"

"As a matter of fact I did, Jake. Awe, I couldn't stand the old bastard; pushing me around, nagging at me all day. As if I'd sold meself to him for thirty bob a week. Well, I got good an' mad an' told him off last evening, and then I quit."

Jake laughed.

"And what you going to do now?"

"Oh, I figured to stick around for a while. That is, if you want me. I can help about the place. I could help Bess in the kitchen, and split the firewood."

"Miriam comes in every day and helps Bess. There, that's her singing outside in the yard now. I guess Glen must be around somewhere. And as for splitting firewood, that gives Glen a chance of seeing Miriam at least once a day. You see, that's the way it is."

"I only thought I would mention it, Jake. You see, I got nothing particular to do all day."

"I thought just now you said you had some mighty important business to take you off."

"Oh, just one or two little things, Jake. I didn't say anything about it being so mighty important, did I?"

Presently Jake said, as though he had been turning it over in his mind all that time: "Sure, pardner, I'll be glad to have you around, if you care to stay."

"You mean that, Jake?"

"You know you don't have any place to go. Might as well stop from now."

"Oh, I could take care of myself."

"I didn't mean it that way, at all."

"So, if you don't really want to have me around – if I would be getting in anybody's way – Look, Jake, I could work the field behind the stables, make a regular garden out of it, that's what I could do."

"That's right, you could do that. Well then, I guess it's all settled. You move in right away. Bess'll fix you up with sleeping. She always agrees with anything I say."

Amos said, grudgingly: "Yes. I guess she's all right."

"A man gets lonely in the days... nothing to do ... no one to talk to. Bess is all right, there ain't a better in the world – but not for talking to, you know that way?"

"I know."

"It's setting up for rain. I can always feel it inside me."

"Always rains August, Jake."

"Another flood like the one we had the year before last and I don't know what the people in this district will do. Drought or flood... anyway you get it in the neck. It beats me to hell, all this..."

"I don't even think about it."

"Just as well."

"I got plenty besides to worry about."

"I bet you have!"

4

Glen took the mare out for a canter across the common. She was acting up frisky, showing her oats. Soon he had her worked up to a nice lather of sweat, and she was going smooth and sweet.

George came down from the house to the edge of the common, sat down on a stone. He watched Glen with envy, and tried to think up a way he could get to ride the mare.

Glen wouldn't let him ride her, thought she was too fractious, and he too young. Glen was like that over some things, a regular mess. He corkscrewed around in his mind to try to think up some device. Nothing gave.

Presently Glen pulled Beauty up from the canter, brought her down to a walk. He walked her over to where George sat on the stone. He was trying to twirl a pimento stick around with his fingers, the way he had seen a man do the other day. He had cut himself a nice straight pimento stick, and stripped all the bark away, and he practised it up regularly. He was coming along fine.

Glen pulled Beauty up to a standstill, and said "Hi!" to George. George grinned back at him and said: "Hi!"

Beauty was restless, she kept jerking at the reins. Glen had to give her half his mind, never knew what she would do.

"Gimme a ride, no?" said George.

"Nothing doing," said Glen. "She'd break your neck, most likely. Shies at anything."

"Man, you never seen me ride," said George.

And Glen said, "We'll save it for another day."

"Was me broke Massa Butty's colt. 'Member?" said George.

"That colt would just as soon broke itself," said Glen. "There's colts and colts."

"Yeh, I know."

"This mare, she's somep'n else again. I'm tellin' you, boy!"

"You ain't tellin' me nutt'n. I can ride any ole mare."

"Yeh?"

"You never seen me ride before."

"All right, we'll save it for another day."

"You not so hot you'self, if it comes to that. Would like to see you broke in a regular buckin' colt."

"You know anymore good jokes like that?"

"Awe hell," said George, "you gimme a crick in the neck."

Glen laughed.

"Give you somep'n else, boy, you don't look out."

"Awe, you gimme corns."

"Anyway I'm just about through exercising her today."

And then the devil gave George a dig in the ribs. He got up off the stone. He took up the stick and started twirling it around his fingers, fast.

He said, his face round and cunning with his devilish intent: "Saw you with Clara Dowson last evening, walking to the wood."

"What's that?" said Glen.

"You heard me, all right," said George grinning impishly.

"All right, you saw me, so what?" said Glen.

"I didn't say anything," said George, and he winked deliberately at Glen.

Glen sat the mare, looking at him with his mouth half-open, he had started to say something, but broke off.

"What's more I ain't saying anything," said George, and he winked at Glen like that again. "Won't nobody hear anything outa me, you gimme a ride, that is."

"Yes?" said Glen.

"You know how it is," said George.

And Glen said, "Yes," again.

"Well, how about it?" said George.

Already his bravado had begun to fail him, seeing that look in Glen's face.

Glen said, quietly: "You had a taste of me belt already, if I remember rightly. You better forget you saw anything, you know what's good for you."

"Awe Glen, I was only joking," said George.

"Yeh. That kind of a joke."

"Was just having a pull at you' leg, you know it. Man, you think I would talk?"

"Don't know if you would talk, who you would talk to, or what you would talk. So you saw me and Clara Dowson last evening, walking toward the wood. And behind what stone or tree you were hiding, sneaking, eh? Suppose you tell me that."

"Wasn't sneakin' on you," said George.

"Wasn't sneakin', eh? I suppose you just happened to be by. Got a good mind give you a taste of me belt, anyway. Jolly well got a good mind."

"Awe, forget it," said George, shifting about uncomfortably. "Forget it, can't you, Glen?"

"Well, you better forget it see? Don't ever let me hear you make talk like that again."

"Was only pullin' you' leg, man. Mean you can't take a joke."

"Joke, eh? That kind of a joke."

He said: "Sometimes you get me worried about you, kid. What kind of a joke you think that is?"

George looked down at his toes and said: "Awe, forget it!" shamefaced. And suddenly he couldn't bear the torment of

Glen's accusation any more. Suddenly he whirled the stick right under Beauty's nose, shouted at her: "Hup, Beauty!"

The mare shied, almost unseating Glen, went tearing across the common, Glen fighting her with the bit.

And now George was really scared.

He didn't know what made him do it.

Now he would get it for sure.

But meantime he just wouldn't be around, no sir! No sense making it too easy for Glen.

5

Bess baked a great big cake.

There was so much batter left over that she had to bake another, smaller one.

The big cake rose so much when she put it in the oven that it split its top, but it came out all brown and smelling so good from the oven, the crack across the upper crust looked just like a great big happy smile.

She started to sing.

And then she remembered about the smaller pan of cake-mixture, and she put that in the oven too.

When it was baked she thought a bit, and remembered about Granny down at the cottage. She would just wrap it up, and send Miriam running down to the cottage, so Granny could have it with her tea.

It wasn't often that Granny got to eat a nice piece of cake like this nowadays, since she had come to stop at the house for the sake of Jake.

So it happened that Miriam was coming back from the cottage when she overtook Clara Dowson just going by the bridge.

She gave her "howdy" quite friendly, and they stopped and exchanged a few words.

When they were parting, Clara said: "How Glen when you see him last? Give him howdy for me."

She went on down the road, singing a little song.

It wasn't anything at all, Miriam told herself, and went on up to the house.

And when she got about twenty yards further up the road she told herself again it wasn't anything.

"A girl can send howdy for a man," she said, "without it being anything."

She put it out of her mind.

*"Dis long time gal Ah never see you,
Come mek Ah hold you' han'…"*

She started to sing.

Presently she broke off singing… that was the same song Clara was carrying with her down the road.

Cho! don't mean nothing at all.

She took a short cut across the common. She must have disturbed a mountain-witch bird nesting on its eggs nearby. It flew into the air with a startled cry.

Down the other end of the common Glen was riding Beauty. The mare was going at full gallop, heading for the wood. He seemed to be fighting hard to pull her in.

Watching that struggle, her heart stood still. Beauty had got the bit between her teeth… she was a brute, that mare. She was heading straight for the wood. She would crack herself up, and him, she wouldn't care.

Glen had said: "Just like a woman, when you cross her, she didn't give a damn!"

They had laughed over it, then; but now she remembered it, she didn't want to laugh.

And then bit by bit Glen fought her head around, put her back up the common again. Going up the hill it was harder, it brought her down to a canter; sobered her up enough for him to bring her down to a prancing, ambling gait.

She smiled way down inside her, knew a sudden feeling of pride. It went warming through her, bringing a glow to her face. She felt so good she started to sing.

"Dis long time gal Ah never see you…"

She broke off at the end of the first line.

What did it matter? A girl could send howdy for a man.

Glen was unsaddling the mare by the stable now. The wind blew cool across the common. It fanned her cheek, brought the glow back to it, thinking of Glen.

What made her start singing like that, going off down the road? Not every minute of the day a girl felt to sing.

It could mean something, as well as it could mean nothing.

And that was as far as she could take it for the time.

6

"How you feeling now?" said Bess, coming into the room, her apron between her hands. "I'm fixing something good for you to eat. I bet you're hungry."

"I'm not hungry," said Jake.

"You always say that."

"It's true, I'm not hungry," said Jake. "Amos is, though. Fix Amos something to eat."

"Sure. I'll fix a bite for both of you."

Came the sound of laughter from without. Bess went across to the window, pulled aside the curtain a crack.

"So much skylarking going on around the place," she grumbled.

"Oh, give them a chance," said Jake. "Miriam's a good girl; so's Glen a good lad. Give them a chance at each other; they're in love."

"Such going's on," said Bess. "I tell you I seen some things happen in my time... a girl has got to be mighty careful with these young fellows around."

She came away from the window reluctantly.

Jake said, suddenly, a note of eagerness in his voice: "Amos is going to live here, Bess. You got to fix up some place for him to sleep."

Bess looked at Amos, and Amos looked away.

"I don't know about that," said Bess. "The house is pretty full as it is. Anyway I suppose I could manage."

Jake laughed.

"That's the stuff. What'd I tell you, Amos? Bess is a good girl. You get on the right side of her, that's all. Rub her down the way the hair lies. Eh Bess?"

And Bess giggled, twisting the end of her apron between her hands.

"You're always joking around."

She went toward the door.

"Well get on with your talking now. I'll be ready for you in just a couple of shakes."

She went through the door.

"You see that, Amos," said Jake. "That's what I mean when I say there are people in life who make it all right, somehow."

"I didn't notice nothing special about her, like that."

"I suppose not. But when you have to depend on people for things... well, that is something else again."

"Now you're talking bitter, Jake. A while back..."

"Yes, a while back...? Why don't you say it, man? I'm full of all the poison of human ingratitude, that's what. I know it, Amos."

"I didn't say anything like that – I didn't mean – "

"Yes, I know. But I'm saying it for you. Why shouldn't I say it? It's true."

"You're too proud, Jake, that's what."

"That, too, yes." He stopped, and said, after a bit: "Proud! ain't that a laugh."

He laughed.

"Jake – " Amos broke off, groping for the right words. They came slowly, the image of what he wanted to say not yet wholly formed in his mind. "You don't let your mind set easy... why you don't let your mind set easy, Jake?"

"That'll come too, I suppose. That – and *rigor mortis*!"

"*Rigor mortis*?"

"It's something that happens to you when you're all fixed for the undertaker," said Jake.

"You got some funny ideas inside your head."

"I guess I have. I can't help it, pardner – any more than you can help not having them, I suppose."

"You don't let anything go *through* you, that's what."

"Go through me? Now that's a funny idea."

"I don't know how to say things like you; but what I mean is everything stops somewhere inside you... you are always fighting everything."

Non-resistance! Amos, you're a philosopher. Did you know that?"

"You can have your joke with me, Jake. I don't mind."

And Jake said, bitterly: "I couldn't, pardner, even if I wanted to."

There was a pause, and then he said: "Estella's back in the district. They won't tell me... they won't tell me anything, but I know it. Never mind how I know."

He got up suddenly. His fists clenched at his sides.

"But I won't see her. I won't have her come here. I couldn't stand to have her pitying me too."

"I don't believe it."

"You're hiding something from me. You're just like the rest of them."

"It's a lie."

"You call me a liar, Amos?"

"It ain't true, Jake. If she was back in the district, I would know it. I pick up things."

Jake sat down again. He changed the subject abruptly.

"A man should have his own life. And a plan. Nothing moves without a plan."

"That's right."

"And then you stop moving; you see how it is? You find you are standing still, caught in a trap, and you can't go forward, nor backward. And what then?"

"What happened to the plan?"

"Exactly. What? You tell me, pardner?"

"I don't know, Jake."

"All right; you start again. Exactly as before. You take the first steps, like it was at the first beginning. But wobbly. Like a man learning to ride a bicycle... Awe hell, Amos, you figure it out."

"You're getting yourself all worked up again. Why don't you give yourself a chance?"

"All the same I won't have her here. She won't ever set foot in this house again. Not as long as I live."

Silence. And then Amos said, clearing his throat:
"Jake, I brought something for you."
"What is it?"
"A tobacco pouch." Putting it into his hand.
"For me?"
"Yes."

Jake didn't say anything for a time, he just kept rubbing his fingers over the leather, as though he was feeling the quality.

"Ten and six I paid for it at the store. And that was special. You couldn't just walk in there and buy it for that over the counter. Genuine pigskin it says on the price-tag. It's still there, I left it on."

"But Amos – ?"
"Well, what's the matter now?"
"It – it's very good of you, but – I couldn't take this."
"Why not? I'm giving it to you. I bought it for you with my own money that I saved up – special for that purpose."

Jake burst out, suddenly: "Why the hell did you have to do that, Amos?"

And Amos stammered, slowly, taken aback: "How – how do you mean?"

"Oh, forget it. I didn't mean anything."
"All right."
"Awe hell, Amos…"
"I think – I understand what you mean. All the same I want you to keep it."
"Sure, pardner. You bet I'll keep it. And thank you."
"No need for that. I wanted you to have it, see?"

There fell a short, embarrassed silence between them. Presently Jake got up. He walked with a curiously uncertain, tentative step, feeling the furniture with his hands. Amos got up quickly and went to him, as though to take him by the arm, but Jake brushed him aside.

"I got to learn to do this by myself."

Amos went and sat down again. He watched the other while he went across to the table where the Bible was lying; he felt over the edges of the book quickly, and took it up.

He came back and sat down again, the Bible in his hand.
"Amos."

"Yes, Jake?"

"Here, take it."

Amos took the book from him.

"What's this for? What's the idea?"

"I want you to read to me."

"Yes?"

"The story of Samson. It's marked at the place. I want you to read the bit where he lost his eyes to the Philistines. Read on till I tell you to stop. Will you do that for me?"

"Yes. Sure, Jake."

He found the place marked in the Bible, cleared his throat, started to read as a man does who is unused to much reading, slowly, haltingly, tracing out the lines with his fingers, sometimes stopping to spell out the words softly to himself.

"*... And they brought him down to Gaza, and bound him with fetters of brass; and he did grind in the prison house...*"

He stopped reading, and looked across at Jake.

"Go on. Can't you manage those words?"

"Yes. Sure."

He went on reading:

"*...and they set him between the pillars. And Samson said unto the lad that held him by the hand, Suffer me that I may feel the pillars whereupon the house resteth...*"

Outside the first great drops of rain began to gather in the sky, they fell heavily against the panes. Amos looked up from the Bible.

He said: "It's going to rain."

And Jake said, impatiently: "Get on with it, man. Can't you read a few lines without stopping every two sentences?"

Amos found the place, and started reading again:

"*And Samson called unto the Lord, and said, O Lord God, remember me, I pray thee, and strengthen me, I pray thee, only this once, O God...* Look Jake, what's the big idea making me read this stuff?"

"All right," said Jake, quietly. "Don't read any more."

"If you want to hear it..."

"No. That's enough. Close the book, Amos."

Amos closed the book, went across to the table and put it down. Bess put her head in through the doorway.

"I've got it all ready, and piping hot. You'll eat in the kitchen, eh?" She stopped, sniffed. "Eh! Now what you two looking so down-in-the-mouth about?"

She came right into the room; went over to Jake.

"Come," she said, gently, "try and take a little soup, even though you're not hungry."

Jake got up, wearily, brushed aside her hand with a gesture of irritation. "All right, Bess, I can manage alone."

He walked a little uncertainly toward the door.

Bess looked after him, shook her head.

"He's just a great big child. Nothing must cross him." She took the end of her apron in her hands, and grinned broadly at Amos.

She said: "Come on and feed your face inside my kitchen."

7

Miriam was tidying up things in the kitchen when Glen came in through the door, carrying the axe across his shoulder. She pretended not to be aware of him. He put the axe down, and came back to where she stood, with her back to him. He was wearing a little shamefaced grin.

"Oh, come on, Miriam. Why don't you act reasonable, eh?"

"What you want me to do?"

"Just be yourself. Quit freezing me off like this."

"Why don't you go to Clara Dowson? Maybe she would act different. The way you would like it."

His brows came together, instantly.

"What's this about Clara Dowson?"

Her heart made like it was a sledgehammer inside her chest, and came back to normal again. Still she said, a spirit of mischief goading her on: "Don't imagine I don't know what's going on behind my back."

"If anyone's been putting you up to anything – " he broke off, suddenly challenged: "Well, what *is* going on? Supposing you tell me."

"You should know."

"Look here, will you quit stalling, and give me a straight answer?"

Her eyes went teasing through him, as she threw him a quick sidelong glance over her shoulder. "I don't want to laugh."

He came up and took her roughly by the shoulders. She struggled to free herself, but gave the show away by laughing. He kissed her quickly on the mouth.

"There, that's better."

She said, feigning anger: "Let me go."

"Don't you like it?" He kissed her again.

"Let me go!"

He laughed confidently as he turned away, crossed over to the opposite wall. He took up the shotgun that was leaning in the corner behind the door, held it absent-mindedly pointing in her direction.

"Put that gun down; it might go off."

"But Miriam, it isn't even loaded."

"Haven't you heard it's always guns that aren't loaded that go off accidentally and shoot people?"

He laughed and put the gun down.

He said: "The birds will be flying over next month."

"Yes, I suppose so."

"What you mean you suppose so? I'm telling you.' He stared reminiscently out the window. "White-wings and bald-pates…"

"Pea-doves and ringtails."

He looked at her in surprise, laughed: "Well, what'd you know!"

The sound of an accordion playing "OLD BLACK JOE" came to them from inside the house.

"Amos is with him. He's going to live here."

"You don't say."

"Can you imagine it?"

But already he had dropped the subject. He came right close to her, and she just stood still watching him warily.

"Look Miriam – "

She shook her head.

"Awe hell, why don't you quit playing around and be serious?"

She saw he was getting angry, and she said, mischievously: "You think I'm not serious enough?"

He stood off a little way and looked at her.

"All right. I guess I'm just a bloody fool after all."

Seeing how it was, she said, a little contritely: "What you want me to do now?"

"I'd like to make you good and sorry, just once."

She gave a little laugh: "Haven't you tried to do that often enough?"

"That's right; laugh. Just because I'm being a sucker about you now –"

"I'm not laughing," she said suddenly, feeling anger rising in her now to answer his.

He said, coming a step nearer: "You think you're going to lead me around with a ring in the nose? Well, get this straight, you nor nobody else ain't never going to do that to me."

"Maybe Clara Dowson… or one of the others. How many of them you have stringing along?"

She didn't know what made her say it; must have been the devil, egging her on.

He said, slowly: "Don't make me get mad and do something I'll be sorry for after."

"You may do something you'll be sorry for after, but not on account of me."

"I'd like to slap your face!"

"What! You must be crazy!"

He laughed.

"You said it. I'm crazy enough to do most anything right this minute. I was crazy enough to tell you that I love you, wasn't I? Well, I'm crazy like that again – only different."

"So you think you were crazy to tell me that!"

"Well, what do *you* think?"

"I think you're crazy now," turning away, "this minute. That's what."

"I've had enough of this. I'm going."

"To Clara Dowson… or which of them? Do you think I'm going to try and hold you?"

"All right. All right."

He went out through the door without looking back.

8

It wanted an hour for dusk; and Glen went down to the river, looking for George.

But George wasn't there. And Glen wasn't too surprised at that.

He went to the same pool and sat down on the same stone where he was that day they saw the strange bird.

He took his face between his hands and started to think.

His anger had left him some time back, and now he just felt a cold dead weight inside him.

He tried to figure out things straight, facing up to the facts.

He still wasn't sure whether George had said anything to Miriam, and somehow it didn't matter any more.

He looked at himself squarely, from inside, and all around.

And when he was finished doing that, he decided he was some kind of a louse, and he wasn't good enough to lick Miriam's shoes.

But it didn't make him any happier.

He chased gals, yes.

The question, whether she knew or not, was of no importance right now.

And there was nothing he could do about it; it was something in his flesh. Like a ping-wing macca that had broken in there and couldn't work its way out again, and it was festering.

He fought against it hard, God knew, but it had him licked from the drop of the cap. Women did that to him. He just couldn't help himself anyhow.

There was Clara Dowson, yes, and others, if she only knew.

Should he go and tell her? Make a clean breast of it? Hell, no, she wouldn't understand.

Women – women like Miriam, that is – couldn't understand about things like that.

God's truth, he wasn't good enough to lick her shoes.

He sat there for a long time, just letting the thoughts go dragging through his mind, without bitterness, anger, resentment, hope, penitence, anything.

He wasn't sorry for anything he had done. Anything he had

done couldn't possibly hurt her, touch her, smirch her. He held her apart from all that.

But there was that, also, that made demands upon his flesh, that his flesh could not deny. And it didn't matter now whether she knew or not. It was past that.

The water went swirling past in its endless repetition of itself. He stared down at it, and it went turgidly on, and on, like his thoughts.

That was how his thoughts went on dragging through his mind. And above them and underneath them he could hear the far faint thunder of the fall.

If she would yield to him, give herself to him, it would make an end of all that. But she held him off, made him keep his distance, yet. And he couldn't hold it against her in his heart.

His thoughts kept on, and on, like the turgid water flowing beneath him.

Girls like Miriam had something to protect. It was more, much more than just their virtue. It went with something else in them that made them carry their heads high. It was neither virtue nor vanity that made them do that, it was something else again that went about the world wanting a name, and men called it this or that, but it meant more and other, and was without a name.

Least that was the way he saw it.

And what it did to him now was to make him feel like some kind of a louse.

But it didn't make him any happier, nor set anything right in his mind.

And presently he got up from the stone he was sitting on, and put his hands in his pockets, and started walking slowly up the path toward the house.

He was staring down at his feet, just setting down one before the other, and the wind brought the sound of voices, and laughter.

They were walking up the same path that went winding over the hill, and they were close together, talking close, like a couple of conspirators, Miriam and George. Like as not coming from another part of the river, further up.

He stood still and watched them until they went over the other side of the hill.

And then he went on slowly, picking his own way home.

9

Amos was taking a little walk alone.

As he went limping by the bridge he saw something white move against one of the white pillars. He stopped and looked. Saw it was Miriam.

He said, "Hello," going up to her. And she gave him a shy smile, and "hello" again.

"You come for a little walk, too?" said Amos.

"Yes. It – it felt kind of stuffy in the house."

"I know what you mean."

"You think it's going to rain some more?"

"Sure to. Later. See how it's making up in the east."

"Yes."

"Rains are about setting-in, I should say. Well, I better be getting along back up to the house."

"No, don't go,' she said, quickly.

"Eh?"

"You could stay a little longer. I – "

"You waiting for somebody, aren't you?"

"Well, not exactly. I just came for a walk." A slight pause. "I – I just want to talk to somebody, if you're not in too much of a hurry."

"I could stay for a while. What you want to talk about?"

"Nothing special. Just talk. It's stuffy in the house. You know that way?"

"Oh yes, sure."

"The moon looks almost double tonight. Funny, ain't it?"

"It's a sign of rain. Going to have bad weather this year, you ask me."

They could hear the sound of people laughing, a far way off, coming up the white road.

A gusty wind started up. It startled the sleeping trees in the wood beyond. The moon put out big from behind a hazy cloud. It sent light twinkling along the leaning grass, and the wind went with running laughter through the trees.

"Ain't it lovely?" she said. "It – it makes you hurt inside." She laughed a little, almost embarrassed. "You know that way."

"Yes."

She looked at him now, thinking about the strangeness of everything. She had never talked with Amos like this before. Before he had just been negative and almost non-existent to her mind. And here she was talking with him as though they had been the closest of friends for years.

She felt a sudden, impulsive warming toward him, she felt she could lay bare her heart to this stranger, who was not a stranger any more.

The gusty wind made risque gestures with her dress about her knees. She laughed, held it down, looking at his face all the time.

She said: "There is something I want you to advise me about."

He shifted uncomfortably from one foot to the other.

He said: "Yes." Like that; but she didn't seem to notice anything, all her attention turned inward, as though it had just passed through the gate, and had its back turned upon what went on outside.

She said, wrinkling up her brows a little: "If a girl should be in love with a young man…" and then broke off, realizing that she had not carefully censored the words in her mind.

Amos's glance went up and down the road. He shifted his weight back to the other foot.

His gaze came back to her face.

She looked so wistful and lost, standing there in the moonlight, that something seemed to stir deep down inside him, moved like an unseen hand putting aside the curtains in a dark room.

"Yes," he said, "go on."

She laughed, embarrassed. Shook her head.

He could guess what was going on inside her mind. Suddenly it announced itself to his own consciousness, as though he had heard an imperative knocking at the gate of the house next door.

It stirred him strangely, making him acutely self-conscious all at once.

He said now, almost gruffly: "You want to talk?"

She didn't say anything, stood staring absently down the white moonlit road.

Her hand lay along the railing of the bridge. Fearfully he put his out, and touched her lightly on the wrist.

He would have pulled away immediately, but her fingers instantly caught and entwined with his. He felt the urgency that went through her, with shrinking, but he held very, very still.

She said, taking the hurdle in her stride: "If a girl should be in love with a young man, should she – let him do things to her?"

She held her gaze purposefully away from his, looking away across the wood. But the clutch of her fingers about his showed where the focus of her attention lay.

They held still like that a moment, and then relaxed a little, and he said:

"It would depend."

"Like how?"

"It's a hard question to answer like that," he said. And then he said, looking at her earnestly, "You love him enough, everything goes, I guess."

She seemed to relax a little.

"I'm so confused."

"Yes."

She looked at him quickly: "You know that way?" laughed, looked away. "You're not a girl," she said. "Men are different… it's – it's different with a girl."

"Yes."

But he didn't say it as though it was the only word in his vocabulary, but quietly confirming it all. And she was satisfied.

She said: "I'm going down to the cottage, Granny's, alone. You going on up the house?"

He nodded. "It will never be the same again…"

"Eh? What you said?"

"Oh, nothing."

"You said, it will never be the same again. What you mean by that?"

"I said that?"

"Yes, you did. What does it mean."

"It can mean about anything, I guess."

But she was suddenly oppressed with this new thought.

"Nothing will ever be the same ... it's – everything is so confusing. Eh? What is a girl to do?"

He started to speak, and then suddenly shut his mouth. From where he stood he could see Bess coming down the road. Miriam's back was turned to her, she could not see.

"Well," she said, giving him a little shake. "You were going to say something, what is it?"

"I didn't say nothing," he muttered, and made to go on.

And then she too saw Bess coming toward them, peering ahead of her narrowly, as she came.

"Oh, it's you, Amos. I thought – "

"Yes, it's me." He was going to add "old scritch-owl!" but thought better of it.

Bess laughed.

"Why you always so huffy?" she said, standing directly in his path. He would have to make a deviation to get around her. He shrugged, stared away across the wood, and started to chew on his lip.

Bess said to Miriam, "You took a little walk-out?"

"Yes, Ma. It was kind of stuffy inside the house."

She nodded, shook herself. "I can feel me clothes sticking to me skin."

Both she and Miriam laughed. Amos grunted, still looking away.

"Well anyway, it's a pretty night out," she said, looking up at the moon.

"Yes, ain't it?" said Miriam. "You going down to the house?"

"Just taking something for Granny, and to tell her howdy, haven't seen her all day."

Miriam turned to Amos. "I will say goodnight now, and thanks for the chat."

He just grunted something and watched them walking together down the road.

When they were out of sight he took his accordion in his hands and started to play.

He played softly, to himself, a tune that came out of his head, making it up as he went along.

In it he was saying all kinds of things, just as the thoughts went through his mind, without stopping to turn them over, just letting them go.

And the melody said what was in his mind, for that was how it was when he played softly to himself like this.

It said, now:

What a lovely miracle this night with moonshine...

The wind laying the grass on its side, laying the little grass...

What a lovely miracle of a night with wind and moon...

Amos, you amount to something now...

And people stop and talk, and pass the time, because they are lonely too...

And nothing will ever be the same again...

Amos, you amount to something now...

Even Jake knows that, even Jake lonely in his darkness in the big house...

So Amos, that surely makes you amount to something now with people wanting to stop you and talk with you for your own sake, because there are lonely people in the world, what a lovely miracle of a night, this night, my God with the wind and the white road before me, and the moon...

10

Jake and Amos sat on the veranda and smoked and talked. It was getting late, but they didn't seem to notice it. There was an electric storm gathering, and the very air around seemed to be subtly charged with electricity.

There was a kind of restless excitement in both of them, but with Jake a note of irritability crept into it. He moved about restlessly, seeming never to be able to stop in one place for long.

Black thunderheads rolled up the sky, and put out the moon.

"What time is it?"

"Must be getting on for midnight, Jake."

"Hum! I don't feel sleepy. Do you?"

"No. Not much."

"You want to turn in?"

"No. Let's sit a while."

"It's going to storm like hell. You feel it?"

"Yes, Jake. It's the weather setting in, I guess."

"I can feel it inside my bones. You scared of lightning, Amos?"

"Er, no."

"Don't lie about it, man, you know you're scared. Nothing to be ashamed of, is it? Why you have to lie?"

"All right, Jake. Don't take on about it."

"Who's taking on, about what? Don't you want me to talk?"

"All right, all right."

"You want to turn in, you can leave me. I'm used to being alone."

"You got any tobacco? Let's smoke."

"There. You see, I'm using the pouch already."

"That's the idea. That's right."

"What's in your mind, Amos?"

"Me? Oh, just nothing at all."

"You're laughing, I can tell that. Don't think you can fool me, pardner, you can't."

"I'm not laughing, Jake. Least, if I'm laughing, it's on account of I'm feeling good, that's all."

"You feeling good, Amos? That's somep'n."

"Yeh, it's somep'n. You said it, man."

"What you feel so good about, Amos?"

"Eh? Oh, things – just things, Jake."

Jake got up suddenly, walked to the end of the veranda, and back.

"What's the matter, Jake, you can't sit still tonight."

"It's lightning already, I can feel it. You scared of lightning, ain't you, Amos? No need to lie about it, you know."

"Yeh, I'm scared, Jake. Just sit down and take it easy, eh? Yeh, I'm good and scared."

Jake laughed. It wasn't a good laugh.

"Damn right, you're scared. Nothing to be ashamed of, man. No need to lie about it, eh?"

"What's on your mind, Jake?"

"There's nothing on my mind special, why?"

"Just thought, perhaps – oh, never mind, forget it," said Amos.

"Okay, forget it, like you say. Where's Bess, she gone inside?"

"Bess must be snoring her head off by now, you want anything?"

"Lend me your matches, can't keep this pipe alight."

"You want anything, I could get it…"

"Don't want anything, man, was only asking where Bess was, that's all."

"You could lend me the matches again? My cigarette's gone dead, too."

"Here, take them. Take them." His hand shook holding out the matches.

Amos looked at him.

"What say we turn in now, eh, Jake?"

"No, no. Wait a little. It's hell, this waiting. Wait up a little bit yet… it's going to storm."

"You – you all right, Jake? You – you sure you don't want anything, I mean?"

"No. Not yet. Not tonight. Just sit. I'll tell you. I give you the matches back, didn't I?"

"Yes. Pipe gone out on you again?"

"Pipe? Oh yes. No. It's drawing fine."

A sudden crash of thunder came with a split and a roar. It seemed to shake the very boards under their feet.

Jake sprang up, crashed against the wall, bounded off again, his hands went clawing along the veranda railing, he was dragging his feet.

"Amos!" he said. And, louder, higher: "Amos!" again.

And Amos sprang up and limped across to him. "Here I am, Jake."

"Don't touch me! Take your hands off. I'll smash you, Amos. You hear."

Amos backed away, involuntarily.

Jake stood with his fists clenched, his face working, his back was to the veranda rail.

He could have hit Amos, heard him breathing heavily where he stood, could have reached him easily in the dark.

His clenched hand came up, seemed to falter, tremble slightly; the intention fused before it reached his fist.

He turned away suddenly. He was trembling all over.

Amos said, quietly: "Jake!"

He didn't answer him the first time.

Amos came a step nearer, and said again, "Jake," quietly, reassuringly, like that.

When he answered it was in a small, smothered voice, like nothing Amos had ever heard.

He said: "God, Amos! I – I could have smashed you, then..."

And Amos said, suddenly, gruffly, "Listen, Jake, you're going inside now. You hear me? I'm taking you inside."

He went right close up to the other, shook him roughly by the shoulder. He couldn't stand to see a strong man cry.

FOUR

Glen was walking along the track through the wood when he saw something flutter across the path.

It was a woman's dress that had caught his eye in that quick flutter across the track, going away into the wood. He stood still and listened now.

Sure enough he could hear the faint sound of twigs cracking underneath her feet.

Somebody playing a prank. He would show them!

He wondered if it was Clara, or which one of the girls. What was she up to, alone in the wood? Why did she run away and hide at his approach?

He would soon find out what she was up to, whoever it was, and maybe give her something she would never forget.

He stepped off the track, started trailing her through the wood.

The noise she made going through the underbush gave her away. Glen couldn't help smiling behind his hand.

She saw him almost as soon as he saw her, and she turned and ran.

The chase ended soon enough. He brought her up, panting, against a tree. She turned to face him, cornered.

She was pretty well finished, done in. If he didn't reach out his arms and catch her she would have fallen to the ground.

He made her sit down, leaning against the trunk of the tree.

He looked down at her, and his face was hard as stone.

"What are you doing here?" he said.

The woman lifted her eyes to his face, imploringly. "Hush!" she said.

He laughed.

"You've got a nerve!" he said. "You don't want anybody to know you're here, sneaking about, is that it?"

She put her hand up to her throat. Her face twisted with a spasm of pain. It passed. She looked up into his face again.

"It's not for myself that I mind," she said, swallowing.

The saliva had thickened in her throat. She had run too fast and too far.

He felt a little pang of pity for her. Nothing more.

"Why did you have to come here, at all?"

"I come here often."

"Why?"

"I don't know. It can't do any harm."

Her fingers started tearing at the short grass beside her. She said presently, without looking up: "How is he?"

"Why do you want to know?" his voice was cruel, hard. "What's it to you?"

He said: "The other one threw you over, that why you come here?"

She turned her head away a little. She didn't answer his question.

She said: "I've got a job in the district here."

He was suddenly, unaccountably angry with her.

"Look here, you keep away from this place. I don't want any trouble with you. You keep clear away from this place, you hear?"

She said, with a note of pleading: "I don't do any harm."

"Women like you do harm just living, just breathing the air other people breathe."

She looked at him now, almost pityingly, he thought, and it made him more angry still.

He didn't stop to reason it out with himself, why he was so resentful of this woman's presence, why he should stand there towering in judgment over her, why the very sight of her defencelessness made him hate her, himself, everyone.

He said: "You shouldn't ought to have come here in the first place. What you want to come hanging around for, eh?"

"I know," she said, and suddenly she seemed to be clothed with calmness and dignity and presence. "Sometimes we do foolish things like that."

He felt abashed, ashamed.

This was crazy, the woman made him feel that he was the trespasser, not she. She looked up into his face again.

"Please don't tell anyone," she said.

He didn't say anything.

And she said again: "Promise me? Please."

"Why should I promise you anything? Look, I don't want to get messed up with this – If Jake was to find out you was coming here, sneaking… well, I don't know what he'd do."

She said quickly, shaking her head: "He mustn't know."

He wanted to turn on his heel and leave her there; what did he want to have words with her for, anyway?

Something held him rooted to the spot, he just stood looking down at her rigid as a tent-peg. "I just can't figure you out at all."

"Don't try. It isn't any use. It doesn't make sense to me, either."

He said suddenly, fiercely: "Why did you have to run away."

"Sit down," she said, indicating a tree stump nearby. "Won't you sit down? I get a crick in my neck looking up for long."

He stood frowning down at her like that, he didn't move.

He felt the initiative had passed from him to her, he felt like a fool, brash, and stupid, and out of his depth. The woman made him feel that way.

He said: "I know I have no right to ask you that."

She shrugged. "What are rights to people like us – you and me?"

He said, coldly: "I don't know what you mean."

"We don't have any rights, like that," she said, "we only have symptoms of possessiveness, that's all."

"I don't know what you are talking about."

"And fits of petulance, when we have lost."

He felt suddenly foolish, even more foolish, standing there.

He went and sat down on the tree stump. He put the fingers of both hands together, and locked them so.

She said, suddenly: "I left him because I loved him, if you want to know."

He looked at her closely, shook his head, his lips curled with a little smile. "You can't mean that."

"Perhaps you're right. Maybe I am a fraud."

"Not that, either."

"What do you know?"

"I am sorry. I shouldn't interfere."

"We're talking. It is good to talk." She said, as though she was turning it over in her mind: "I loved him, yes. I wanted us both to have a chance."

"You had yours." The bitterness crept back into his voice again.

"You think I ran away lightly, for a thrill?"

"I wouldn't know."

"You are in love, perhaps," she said.

He moved uncomfortably.

"That is different. A man is different. Besides – "

She said, fiercely: "I didn't want to have him on my hands so much. I wanted he should have his chance."

"I don't understand you," he said, coldly.

He said: "A hell of a way to go about it, just the same."

"All right, I shouldn't have said it. Forget I ever said it, please."

"You said just now, we didn't have any rights, only symptoms of possessiveness, what do you mean?"

"If you were in love you would know."

"Why don't you keep away," he said, suddenly, "what's the sense your coming here?"

"Perhaps I'm haunted," she said, and he could see she wasn't joking.

"Haunted?"

"Yes. Like the ghost of the old man who hanged himself from the cotton tree."

"You – you shouldn't say a thing like that."

"Why not? If it's true."

But she wasn't listening to him; her fingers were plucking at the grass beside her.

"Maybe I wanted to make sure, for myself. Maybe that too, but – I can't be certain any more."

She laughed, pulling some more grass with her hands.

"I ran away from the other too, you know."

She said, looking straight into his eyes: "He didn't beat me, or anything. Only, with him, I was sure."

2

Bess was cobwebbing the room, and Jake was sitting over by the window in a patch of sunlight, his hands folded in front of him. He might have been asleep.

How she managed it she didn't know, but she knocked the shotgun off the bracket against the wall.

It fell to the floor with a racket, and Jake sprang to his feet.

"Good God, Bess! Be careful, can't you!" he shouted at her.

She just stood there with her hand over her heart.

When she could speak, she stammered: "It's the spider. I – I killed one of them spiders the other day."

"That's no reason for you to go knocking things down."

He turned angrily back to the window, sat down, folded his hands in front of him, as before.

She was on the verge of tears, but she was too scared even to let them go. And then Amos came into the room. She didn't know when she had ever been so glad to see anyone. When he was in one of these moods, there wasn't no one but Amos could do anything with him.

Amos just glanced about the room now, limped over to where the gun lay, took it up, broke it to see if it was loaded, found it was not, hung it back on its bracket against the wall.

Her eyes followed him all the way across the room, and then she turned and went heavily on tiptoes through the door.

Amos went across to the window.

"How you feeling, Jake?" he said.

Jake grumbled something, and Amos said: "You want Miriam to come and read to you?"

"No. Just want a little quietness, that's all."

"All right, Jake."

He pulled up a stool and sat down beside him. He rolled himself a cigarette and started to smoke.

"It's beginning to look like a garden at last, Jake," he said, taking a deep drag at his cigarette, and blowing the smoke out again.

Jake just sat with his hands folded in front of him, he didn't say anything at all.

"Wish you could just see it," said Amos. "I planted a patch of them okras up against the stable wall, just like you wanted. They're putting out blossoms already, what'd you know!"

He sat silent for a moment, just staring out in front of him too, and presently he got up and went across to the place where the gun hung on the wall.

"What you doing there, Amos?"

"Nothing, just thought I'd take the gun and clean it."

"Let it be, man, let it be."

Amos looked at him, shrugged, turned away.

He said, at the door: "I'm going out again, unless you want me."

"All right," said Jake, "just close the door as you go through."

Amos said, casually, his hand on the door: "By the way them things came in the post yesterday, the modelling clay and the stuff that goes with it."

"Yes, I know."

"Don't you want me to send them in for you?"

"Maybe, yes. Some time."

Amos hesitated at the door a moment longer, then he stepped out into the passage and drew it shut behind him softly. He was shaking his head as he limped down the passage toward the outer door.

3

There was another thunderstorm that evening, and the rain really set in.

It rained like that steadily for days.

The whole countryside was flooded out. People's houses, cattle, crops, were carried away.

Already there was starvation in the district; road, rail and telegraphic communication didn't exist any more. They were cut off, marooned from the rest of the world. Already epidemics had broken out.

But above and beyond all this there was something for rejoicing as far as Amos was concerned. He had made an important discovery.

Jake wasn't scared of the lightning any more.

It meant so much to Amos, it meant that Jake was coming the long road, back again. Only give him time – he would come all the way.

He and Bess were in the living-room now, talking, and he overlaid his great joy with an irritation that he did not altogether feel.

"People dying everywhere! It's a hell of a world," he said.

"It's God's doing. We mustn't murmur."

Amos turned on her: "That's foolishness. What's the sense there is a God, if he is to send flood-rain to drown poor people, and their crops and cattle and everything? To leave them without providing of any sort – neither food nor shelter, and to send sickness among them. What's the use?"

"There's things we don't understand."

"*You* don't, you mean."

Bess got on to a new theme.

"There's not a blessed stick of firewood in the place. We'll have to turn around and start burning the furniture next."

And Amos said: "We're of no more count than the ants under our feet."

"Life begins for me on a Monday morning, every blessed week. It's always been like that… like as if it was beginning all over again, every seven days."

"It's the weather," said Amos. "When it rains like this I don't even know what day of the week it is."

"You're hungry. You better eat something."

"What's there to eat?"

"Bread and cheese."

"That's plenty. Think of some of those poor devils out there."

She took a loaf of bread and some cheese from the safe, and set them on the table before him. He drew up, and started to eat.

"Aren't you going to have some yourself?"

"Not even a bite. It would stick in my gullet. I'd give my eyetooth for some pumpkin soup, though – hot."

"What you been eating all these days past?" he said, with his mouth full.

"That's just it. Bread and cheese."

"You ought to be thankful we have that."

"Bread, green with mould on it, and hard as a stone... and cheese the same."

"Think of all those who don't even have that."

"As far as I can remember, I've always had a fire going in my kitchen."

This time it was Amos who changed the subject.

"What's happened to Glen, I wonder?"

"Hm! Hasn't set his foot in here for the past three days. That's the sort of man my child goes gallivantin' with."

"I bet it isn't Miriam's fault."

"What do you know about it, anyway?"

"What do *you* know, if it comes to that!"

"Amos Gladstone, if I didn't know what's going on around my own child, I wouldn't be a natural woman."

"They had a quarrel, eh? And you think she's in the wrong."

"I never said anything of the sort. Don't you try to twist my words."

"Trouble with you, you don't realize Miriam's growing up. You ought to be glad about that, 'stead of acting the way you do."

"If she knew what *I* knew at her age, she'd be well and able to hold her man. And let's have no nonsense about it."

"Perhaps she doesn't want to hold him. Maybe she got other ideas."

"Yes? Then what's the sense her crying her eyes out about the place then, tell me that?"

"You mean that, eh? She doing that? Oh!"

"So on account of she wants to have her high and mighty airs, we don't have *that* of wood to make a fire with." She made a gesture with her fingernail and thumbnail together.

"If you bring that up again, I'll go out meself with the axe, and get drowned coming across the river maybe."

She said, quickly: "No you don't, you stay right here. I wouldn't be left alone to be responsible for *him*!" With a jerk of her head in the direction of the bedroom.

"M-m-m!" Amos mumbled, but he didn't say anything.

"So you just stay right where you are. Would you like some new-sugar beverage with your bread and cheese?"

"Don't bother."

She said, "No bother at all," going toward the kitchen. From inside the kitchen she said: "Red ants all over the floor!" And when he didn't make any comment: "Are you there?"

"Yes, I heard you. Red ants, you said. What to do?"

Presently she came back with an enamel mug of beverage, taking something out of it with a spoon. "In the sugar and all. And it's stood in water. Must be they swim! It was the same the year before last. Only it's worse this time."

Amos said, mischievously: "Hush you' mouth, it's God's rain."

"Don't blaspheme, Amos Gladstone."

"I'm not blaspheming, was I? I only said..." he was speaking with his mouth full, and suddenly choked.

"Watch you don't choke yourself. Would serve you right."

He swallowed hard. "Well, quit grumbling then."

She sat down at the table, took her apron between her hands. "I know I shouldn't ought to. It's God's doing, we mustn't murmur."

Amos said: "Everybody's got troubles. Don't I know it? Still and all..."

Bess brought a finger up to her lips and leaned forward. She whispered: "I feel he's listening all the time... just like he don't trust us anymore."

Amos said, quickly: "Don't say it, Bess."

He chewed slowly on the bread and cheese in his mouth, swallowed some of the beverage from the mug. "He thinks we're spying on him, if you want to know. But it's nothing, it'll pass. Just give him a chance, he'll come to himself again."

"He don't trust us, and we're his friends. After all we been through on account of him."

Amos said sharply: "Who's been through what?"

"I only said..."

"Well, you leave me out of it. Speak for yourself."

"You talk as though I said something terrible bad."

"Seems to me like you did. Do you feel that sorry for yourself, then?"

She brought her apron up to her eyes. "I didn't mean anything like that."

"You shouldn't say it then."

"You pick up every word that drops out of my mouth. Sometimes you make me frightened to talk." Her voice broke and she started to weep.

He said, harshly: "Cut that out!"

"I believe you hate me. I – I wouldn't be surprised."

"Don't start that foolishness. I don't hate anybody."

"Ain't nobody, but one, you ever think of at all."

"I don't fancy messing myself up with people, if that's what you mean."

"There you go again, everybody else is just '*people*'!"

"All right, all right, don't start all that over again."

"I do believe you hate me, that's a fact."

"And I believe you're crazy. So we're quits."

But Bess had to get in the last word: "Say what you like, if it wasn't for him you wouldn't be nobody, nobody at all. You can't be somebody being all to yourself, like that. You've got to let yourself go among people; even if it hurts you to do it."

"All the same I don't aim to get mixed-up too much with people. All the same."

"Don't you believe it! You're just as sentimental as anybody else. Think you can fool me? You're just afraid."

"Who's afraid, of what? Who's trying to fool anybody? I never said I wasn't…" And then he forgot what he was going to say.

"All right then, you didn't say anything. I'm just a mind-reader."

"You're talking about Jake. 'Bout Jake and me. I get you." He broke off. "Well, I owe Jake something, don't I?"

"So does he owe you, and plenty, too. No sense pretending about it."

"I don't see it that way," Amos said gruffly. "Let's talk about something else, eh?"

"All right, then, let's talk about the weather."

"Clever, eh?"

"There you go again! I suppose there's something under the sun we can talk about."

He said, mimicking her: "If only we had some nice dry firewood, we could make a nice little fire." She gave him a stony stare.

Amos turned his face in the direction of the bedroom door, as though he had heard a sound of movement within.

"It's bad him not coming out of his room for a whole day, Bess – and not wanting anyone near him, either."

"He thinks too much, that's what."

"You said it. It's not good a man should think so much... about some things, anyway."

She looked at him closely. "You love him, don't you?"

He didn't reply, just sat scowling at her across the table. She looked down at her hands.

And then he said, slowly: "He's been a powerful good friend to me, Bess."

"What he ever done for you?"

"Don't ever talk like that. And you too – you ought to be ashamed."

"Never mind. I guess I'm a bit upset, that's what."

After a while Amos said, musingly: "Sometimes I'm afraid..." and left it like that.

"Yes. I know. We've got to be very watchful. I've had the same feeling myself."

Suddenly Amos blurted out: "Bess, God forgive me – it's not him I'm afraid for so much, but for myself."

"What do you mean?"

"You asked me just now what he done for me. I'll tell you. He's given me my life again, as a man. Do you understand what I mean? Now I have something. I have him now, to lean on me."

"I think I understand what you mean."

His voice came scarcely above a whisper: "I used to think how folks would stop and stare. And maybe they would say 'howdy' to me, passing in the street... folks would stop me in the street and speak to me. They would want to shake my hand."

Jake came stumbling out of the room.

"Amos, are you there? It's so dark everywhere. Inside and outside too. And nothing stirs in the darkness. Christ! It's like being dead – and alive to know it. Amos. Amos, where are you?"

Amos went to him quickly, "Here I am, Jake."

His hand gripped his shoulder till it hurt.

He said, "Yes."

And then he turned and went inside again.

Amos limped back to the table. Suddenly he had lost all his poise. He said, fidgeting with his hands: "Can't we get a fire started at all? Can't we manage somehow? Isn't there anything we could burn?"

And Bess said, tearfully: "Only the furniture. I done burned up everything else them last two days. Down to an old box and a broom I had in the kitchen, for standing on and sweeping down the cobwebs with." The apron came up to her face again. "I'm willing to work my fingers to the bone, without a word of complaining, but the Lord Jesus knows I can't make a fire without wood."

Jake stood silhouetted in the doorway, but neither of them noticed this.

Amos said, "If we could make a fire it would be something to do. It would be cheerful; take our minds off all this."

"There's the axe where Glen left it, over in the corner by the window. What you going to do, rip up the floor?"

They went into the kitchen together.

Bess said, fretfully: "Nothing but ashes all over the place. Soot and ashes everywhere. And ants!"

"I'll get some newspaper," said Amos.

"Newspaper alone can't make a fire."

He sat down.

"Wait, we got to figure something out."

He said presently, as though he had arrived at a solution: "Hell then, we won't have a fire! What we want to start a fire so almighty important for, anyway?"

"Was you who said we should have a fire."

"Well, never mind about it. I guess we can manage without. There's plenty a sight worse off than us today."

She said, leading the way back into the living-room: "Yes, poor things. I can think of one, especially."

"Who's that?"

"A woman who left her husband some months ago." She brought her hand up to her mouth, made a funnel of it, whispered hoarsely: "She's back in the district again, I hear."

"The worthless trash! May lightning strike her!"

"Hush! you mustn't say that."

"Why not?"

Bess shook her head: "You don't know what she's suffered. Nor me, neither. We shouldn't judge her."

"Suffered! Well, she isn't coming here to torment him, not if I know it."

"I don't think she means to do that, anyway."

"What she come back for then? Why don't she stay where she was – with her fancy man?"

"She's left him."

"And now she wants to come back, I suppose."

"I don't know about that. You don't understand the heart of a woman, Amos."

"No. Thank God!"

There was a bright flash of lightning, and answering thunder. Amos went across to the window.

"I believe the weather is breaking."

"Praise be to God!"

"What's that?" suddenly, unbelievingly. "Good God!"

Bess ran to the window to see what it was. They both drew back a little, and looked at each other.

And Bess said, just above a whisper: "When did he go out?"

"Take it easy, now. We don't want him to think we're spying on him, remember."

They turned away from the window and sat down again, and Jake staggered in through the door. His boots were muddy. He was carrying a heavy sack over his shoulder. He set it down.

Bess said, conversationally: "The weather is breaking."

And Jake laughed and said: "Lightning and thunder. Yes."

He said, coming a little further into the room: "But you never saw such lightning, Bess."

"Eh?"

"It's black... like my hand before my face." He waved his hand before his sightless eyes. There followed an awkward pause.

"Black lightning."

Amos said, uneasily: "What's that you got there, Jake?"

He answered in one word: "Firewood."

He went into the bedroom, closed the door.

Amos went quickly to the sack, opened it, looked in. He closed the neck of the sack, and looked at Bess.

"I guessed it from the moment he stepped in."

"What is it?"

"Samson. It's his carving that he never had a chance to finish." He said, quietly: "It's finished now."

Bess started weeping softly in her apron: "Oh God, save us!"

"And that's not all. There's more to come."

FIVE

Sun rolled up the sky.

The dark clouds were folded away, the sky was blue all above, with just enough washed-out clouds, and thin, with the edges misty and serrated like the foliage of a tree... the weather had broken, not a doubt about it... some light showers yet to come, but not enough to spoil a fine day.

The trees stood tall and still like a regiment of soldiers come to rest, at ease, at the edge of the wood.

The close grass that hugged the contours of the valley had a bluish tinge to it, nourishing itself secretly on the rich silt and the moisture from the leached hills and slopes above, and here and there little clusters of yellow flowers came out with a bright flame of colour among the close blue grass.

There was not enough wind here to move anything, except where the switchlike sticks of wild sage held up heads of purple and orange that were sly annotations of colour that the roving eye might miss, merging with the pattern about it where the common made margin with the sombre wood.

And beyond those the blue hills, and beyond the hills the mountains, their slate-coloured peaks showing like islands among the mist, crisp now, and thriftless, without the threat of moisture and humidity to make them let down in sudden peevish rain.

Work on the new job was going on up at the blacksmith's shop. Glen, who was in charge now, had got him an assistant, a young man of about his own age, named Uriah. George still helped with the bellows, as usual, and did odd jobs about the place.

The coal in the forge came to a bright ruby glow under the brisk manipulation of George at the bellows, and the lump of pig-iron on the forge turned sullenly from ashen grey and took on gradually the colour that was at the heart of that breathing, smouldering huddle of coal.

Then the lump of pig-iron was hoisted from the forge and laid on the great anvil, and work with the hammers started. The hammers beat out a rhythmic pattern made up of quick and slow strokes, and the leader by the pattern and measure of the tattoo he beat could communicate to his assistant when he should withhold his own hammer strokes, because it was enough.

And so the rhythmic strokes ceased suddenly, altogether; and Glen hefted the piece of pig-iron in its new shape off the anvil, and plunged it into the iron drum of water which stood to one side waiting to receive it.

A sweet young heifer, trailing a rope from around its neck, put her head in inquisitively at the door of the shop and mooed complacently. Her great brown eyes sought for and found George and held him for a long time in her wistful, gentle gaze.

Glen looked up and said: "George."

And George grinned, and said, unabashed: "I tied her out good and strong, Glen, I swear I tied Betsy out. Lookit she is wearin' the rope around her neck and everything."

"You better go and tie her out again," said Glen, quietly. "And this time see that she don't get a chance to loose that rope herself, or else maybe you'll be feeling a taste of my belt."

"Okay, Glen," said George; he whistled going up to Betsy and taking her head under his arm, affectionately.

She tossed her head playfully, as though she would throw him, but George only knuckled her forehead a bit with his other hand, and said, gently, "Good old Betsy; come to look for me, eh old girl?"

He took the end of the rope in his hand, and said, "Come."

She followed him like a dog.

Uriah chuckled.

He said: "He sure has a hand for animals. Don't it now?"

"Yes," said Glen. "He has the touch."

"All the same," said Glen, "he's not going to ride Beauty. Not yet."

"Eh?" said Uriah, looking at him.

"Nothing," said Glen. "I didn't say anything at all."

Uriah said: "Okay. Let's get on with the job."

"We not going any further with it today. I want to get some particulars about it first. We do something now, maybe we got to do it all over."

Uriah had left, and Glen was about locking up the shop when Miriam sauntered down the hill like she was going past. She carried a little basket over her arm, because she was going to pick limes off a tree that grew beside the pass that went to the river.

She had every mind to pass without stopping, but something made her look in at the shop, and their eyes met in a challenging glance, and an imp of mischief woke in her.

She came casually up to the door now and stopped. She said: "Howdy," rather primly, and then, "Where is George?"

"Somewhere about the place, you looking for him?"

"Not special."

She stood teasingly in the doorway, swinging the basket over her arm, her lips gathering into a slight, tight smile. He looked at her, warily, searching in his mind for words. His thoughts about her teased him. He thought, maybe she wants to make friends; maybe she wants to stop and talk. And then; what she want to stop for, anyway? She's up to some mischief, you may bet. She wants to see if she can get a rise out of me. Well let her try.

"You locking the shop early," she said.

He said: "Huh."

"Well, I was just passing," she said, "going down the river pass to pick some limes."

He looked at her, but his eyes gave nothing away; he was not buying anything, they said.

She wanted to drop all pretence, let down her reserve and plead with him, she didn't know how, or for what.

She said, with a bright laugh: "Well, are you just going to stand there and not say anything?"

"You said you were going to pick limes down the river pass."

"Yes," she said. And then she said, quickly: "I – I wasn't asking you to come."

"I didn't think you were. Did I say that?"

"I'm just telling you," she said.

"You just stopped to tell me that."

"What you mean?"

"Nothing. I'm just wondering, that's all."

"Mind you don't wonder something wrong."

And somehow the words didn't ring right. They did not say what she had meant to say at all. She felt suddenly confused, and a little helpless and short-circuited. She laughed, a bright hard laugh.

What was it that was always confounding them, when – when it could be so different, he thought; and he started to say, "Miriam…" with the thought of what he wanted to say as yet unformed in his mind.

"Yes? What?"

"Oh, nothing. I was just thinking."

"What were you thinking about?"

But the thought still eluded him – no, the thought was there, but the words – the words came stuck together in his mind.

He shook his head, looked away, out through the window at the sombre wood.

"Nothing. I forget."

"Oh."

She laughed again, and she didn't want to, and she knew it didn't sound right, but it was out already, and she couldn't catch it back.

He turned from looking through the window, and stared at her hard. A muscle was moving in the side of her throat, the way it did when she was getting angry.

Anger to match hers mounted slowly inside him; and suddenly he resented her coming here and making a fool out of him, getting him all mixed-up, so that he couldn't get his thoughts straight, but struggled with his words, couldn't get them to say what he wanted to say.

"Well, I was just passing," she said.

He just stood looking at her, and didn't say anything at all.

"I am sorry I disturbed you," her voice was crisp and stilted, "you don't seem to want to talk."

He felt now he must say something.

"What you want to talk about?" he said.

"Me?" she opened her eyes wide upon him, "I didn't say I wanted to talk about anything special."

She looked away and shrugged, took two steps toward the door, going away.

"Miriam – "

She looked at him over her shoulder.

"Yes? You want to say something?"

He blurted out: "What you came here for in the first place?"

She turned again to face him fully; her eyes blazed at him: "Eh?"

He wanted to take two steps toward her, gather her in his arms, tell her he didn't mean anything of what he said, tell her of the torture of mixed-up emotions that had him swinging around in circles until he was dizzy. But those two steps between them yawned like a fixed chasm. He couldn't get his muscles to obey his mind, as though they had an independent will of their own, and a warning the gesture would be rebuffed.

George's cheery whistle broke in on the silence that lay between them.

Glen grinned with sudden relief, as though he was conscious of reserves coming to his assistance. "There's George now," he said.

And she said, "Thank you, I can find my own company without any help from you," turned and walked away, swinging the basket on her arm.

George said: "You want, I could finish locking up." There was the ghost of a twinkle in his eye.

"Go to the devil," said Glen.

George said, cheerfully: "Okay."

He went whistling toward the door.

"Where are you going?" said Glen.

"My business," said George.

"Don't give me any of your cheek," said Glen.

And George said: "Okay, boss," and grinned.

Glen picked up a hammer and swung it like a pendulum. Then he let the hammer drop to the ground. He sat down, and made up his lips to whistle, but no tune came. George went across to the window and started to bar it.

Glen said, without looking at George: "She's gone down the river pass to pick limes. You better go help her. That lime tree is full of prickles, you better go on down and help her."

George said, quietly: "Why you don't go yourself?"

Glen looked at him now, but George turned a straight face to him.

"Go on and do like I say," said Glen.

George went out through the door.

Alone in the shop now, he sat for a long time looking down at his hands. His elbows rested on his knees, and his big hands just hung down loose between them. He sat staring down at them a long time like that.

His shoulders gave a little twitch of themselves, and he got up. He put his arms above his head, locked his hands together, and stretched up. His lips formed into a wry smile.

He went over and barred the window on one side, and then on the other.

He took a jack knife from his pocket, opened it, started whetting the blade on the palm of his other hand. He reached down and picked up an old shingle and started whittling at it. He pulled up a stool over to the door, sat down on it and went on whittling at the old shingle.

He sat like that for a long time, and the silence grew around him, and he was lost in his own thoughts.

2

Miriam came to where the lime tree grew at the edge of the pass. She looked at it, and it looked back at her, and it seemed to her ugly and leering. It just thrust out its thorns at her, and stood there, waiting.

"Wicked old lime tree," she thought, "just like an old witch."

She went up to the tree and started picking the limes that were within easy reach of her fingers. Then she reached up and took one of the branches in her hand and pulled it down to her, and her hand slipped somehow and a thorn went deep into her hand, and broke off when she let go.

She put her hand to her mouth and shut her eyes tight, her teeth clenched about the broken ragged end of the thorn. Then she held her breath and pulled hard, and the thorn came away, and a trickle of blood came with it.

She sucked at the wound but that only made it bleed more, and presently she sat on a stone under the tree, and took a smaller round stone in her good hand and started beating the other hand with it. She did that to stop the bleeding.

The trickle of blood became less and less, but her hand ached, and staring at it, holding it on her lap, loose, like that, she heard whistling coming down the track, looked up, and saw George coming toward her.

"You got a prickle in your hand," he said.

He reached down and picked up a smooth round stone and handed it to her. "Here, you beat it with that."

She said, pulling a wry smile: "I beat it already."

"It hurts," she said. "It hurts like hell."

And he said: "Yes. It always hurts like that."

He squatted down beside her, took up a piece of stick and started drawing a face on the ground.

She felt miserable, and as though she was going to start crying any minute now, and she shut her eyes tight and held her throbbing wrist.

He said: "You put some salt on it when you go up to the house. That will draw out anything that is in it."

She didn't say anything.

He drew in the eyebrows in the face with the sharp end of the stick, whistling softly all the time through his teeth.

"You know somep'n?" he said, and without waiting for her answer, "the two of you gimme a crick in the neck."

"Eh? What you say?"

"Say you gimme a crick in the neck."

"What you talking about?" she said.

"Don't you know?"

"No, I don't, or I wouldn't ask you; what's it?"

George stood up and flung a stone at a bird in a tree limb across the pass.

He said, changing the subject abruptly: "I whistle to Betsy

now and she come to me, you don't believe it?"

She didn't say anything, and he turned and faced her again and said: "Suck it."

"Eh?"

"You suck it good and hard it'll stop hurting so much, prickles have poison in them, didn't you know?"

She said: "Oh,' and brought the injured hand up to her mouth.

"Goin' pull some of that Spanish Needle for Betsy," he said.

He went a little way off where some tall weeds grew, started pulling them up with his hands.

A gold and green banana bird flew into a tree overhead, and he stopped pulling at the weeds to look at it.

He whistled to the bird, and the bird cocked an eye to look at him, and whistled a few notes.

He put both hands on his head, turned his face up, and whistled to the bird so that you couldn't tell which was the bird and which was the boy.

The bird took three little hops along the limb, seemed to hesitate, and then flew away to another tree.

George laughed. "You can't fool birds. They got plenty sense."

She forgot about the pain in her hand now, and all the misery that seemed to come to a point of focus with it.

She said: "You whistled just like the bird. You would fool me."

With his hands still on his head he turned and looked at her, then looked away.

"Them little beany-birds got sense," he said.

3

Jake sat on a chair pulled up to the window, his sightless eyes staring straight out in front of him. He was whittling on a piece of stick, to give his hands something to do, the better to endure the loneliness and the darkness that had settled upon his life.

Amos found him like that when he came into the room.

He carried a big melon in his hands; came over to the window with it.

"Look, Jake. Gee, get a feel of it."

"What's it?"

"A melon, man. Come out of the garden."

"Huh," said Jake, and that was all.

"It's 'most as big as me," said Amos, with a laugh. "Melon got more meat on it, though."

He laughed as though he was thoroughly enjoying the joke.

"People should see me carrying a melon like that they'd stop and stare. They'd say, where that big melon goin' with that little man? Ha, ha, ha!"

"I tell you what," he said, "let's cut into it before ole Bess finds out."

"You go ahead, Amos, I don't want any."

"What, you don't like melon, Jake?"

"Not hungry," said Jake.

"Look, Jake, if you could just see the thick red meat – if you could just – just bite into it…"

"Don't feel for any just now," said Jake.

"Ah well," said Amos.

He drew up a stool near to the window and sat down.

He tried to figure a way to fight this mood of despondency that had settled upon Jake, but without success. He took a piece of string from his pocket and started making two of diamonds with it.

"What's on your mind," said Jake.

"Nothing," said Amos. "Making two of diamonds with a piece of string, Jake, you know it?"

Jake shrugged impatiently, and Amos put the piece of string back in his pocket.

"What you want to do, Jake?" he said.

"Eh?" said Jake.

"You want me to read to you, or something?"

"Leave me alone," said Jake.

Amos didn't say anything for a while, and then he said, quietly: "All right, Jake. Anything you say."

"Don't say that."

"Eh?"

"You don"t start treating me like a child now. It's bad enough with Bess."

"I'm sorry, Jake. Didn't mean to."

"Awe, forget it."

Time went on to the count of a full minute.

Presently Jake said: "It's stopped raining. The weather's broken."

"Yes."

"You know something, Amos, I have a fancy to take a walk in the wood."

"Yes, that would be fine, Jake. You would like that. That would be just grand, when it gets a bit drier."

"Yes."

"Couple of days from now it'll be grand in the wood again."

"Eh?"

"What we were talking about, Jake…"

"Awe, forget it."

"I thought you said…"

"Awe, forget it."

The clouds made like cut-out paper patterns that were pasted against the sky. A flock of cling-clings flew across the common, they came to rest in a nearby tree. They called to each other among the branches with the sharp, twanging notes of a steel guitar.

"The worms are coming up out of the ground," said Jake, as though he was turning over the thought in his mind.

"Eh? Oh yes, the worms."

"The cling-clings are waiting for them to come up into the light… they sit and talk to each other, waiting, in a tree."

"Yes."

"Life's a funny business," said Jake.

"You said it, Jake."

"What I said?"

"That about life, you know."

"Didn't say anything. Was thinking, that's all."

"Yes. You was thinking aloud, I guess."

Jake just made a little movement with his shoulders. He didn't say anything at all.

"You know somep'n funny?" said Amos, "you an' me sittin' here, talkin' the things we talk."

"What's funny about that?"

"Er, I don't know how to say it."

Jake said, irritably: "Amos, you're a bloody fool."

"I guess we all say foolish things sometimes," said Amos.

"Yeh," said Jake, "I guess we do."

Amos made as though he was going to ease himself off the stool. He sat down again, shook his head, looked down at his empty hands, palms upwards, put them away inside his pockets, stared out through the window; tight lines drew up one side of his face.

If only he could think of something to lift that cloud of despondency that had settled upon Jake. A man couldn't drag himself into a corner, and live alone, in the dark. And that was what Jake was trying to do.

He got up off the stool now, and went across to the table where his accordion lay. He took it up and came back and sat down on the stool again, and started to play.

He made up the music as he went along, and it went with his thoughts as they thronged through his mind. And it went like this:

The storm is past, and all is smiling in the world again,

Little wind making sport upon the common with the grass, and all...

A man can't take himself off into a dark corner somewhere in the world and love it,

Not too much love it, a man can't...

A little love must go with everything in the world, otherwise it gets too lonely

And a man can't bide too much loneliness, and without any little love at all.

Little clouds making dance against the sky, the storm is past...

Cling-clings sing to each other across the common from calabash-gourd to guava tree...

Sun looking over a high cloud takes the measure of the day... and holds his two sides laughing...

What so weary in all the world as a man sitting in a corner alone, eating his heart out in darkness...

4

George went whistling toward the stable carrying a bundle of sweet young grass under his arm. He stood in front of the draw rails and fed it by the handful to Beauty.

He talked to her in a low, caressing voice.

"Nice girl, Beauty... bring you sweet guinea grass... like it, hey? ...goin' ride you some day, Beauty, girl... goin' ride you a gallop across the common some day... Glen, he don't know nothing at all... both of them the same, don't know nothing at all... don't know what they want, even... not like you an' me, Beauty, ole girl... we know what we want... we want to go a gallop across the common... go like the wind, eh girl, don't it... you eat you' belly full, got plenty-plenty more... bring you nice sweet young guinea grass everyday... love it, eh?... all right then, you eat you' belly full..."

He put one foot up on the bottom draw-rail, and as Beauty tore at the tender grass he put his free hand up and rubbed the white star in the centre of her forehead. The mare put back her ears, but the boy only laughed, "You like it, I know... you like pettin', don't it?... can't fool George, you know, ole girl... got plenty more sense than that... some day goin' bridle you, take you out, mount you, an gee, we'll go a gallop across that ole common... you bet!... eh Beauty, girl?... ha, ha, you bet!... go on, then, take it... eat all you can... I bring it for you, didn't I?... you eat you' belly full..."

Dusk sifted across the valley, the wind moved among the trees. Far off there was the dim murmur of the fall.

Beauty snorted, lifted a foreleg, pawed the stable floor.

George whistled softly between his teeth, scratched Beauty behind the ear. The mare tossed her head, and then her head came down again, and she held still.

George whistled softly and scratched that little place behind her ear. She rested her head against the top draw-rail, stretched it out.

George stopped whistling and grinned a little. Her breath was warm and tingling against his cheek.

5

Bess was in the kitchen getting supper ready. She was having trouble with the fire, and smoke had got into her eyes. She rose heavily from kneeling down in front of the fireplace, puffed, and fanned her apron before her face.

She muttered something about "That girl…" and, "take a stick to her one of these fine days…"

Bess had formed the habit of talking to herself like that when she was alone. "For the sake of company," Miriam said, "Ma just hates for nobody to hear her at all." It made Amos laugh when she said it. He said, "You got spunk, child; takes spunk to live longside of your Ma."

She was still wiping tears out of her eyes from the smoke with her apron when George came in carrying a bundle of firewood. He put it down in the wood bin.

Bess went across to the wood bin grumbling to herself, and as she put her hand in to take some of the wood a lizard jumped on her arm.

Her voice went suddenly small and shrill on her.

She said weakly, "Get it off! Get it off!"

George grinned, picked the lizard off with his fingers.

She sat down weakly, stared at him aghast.

When she could catch her breath she said: "You mean you just stand there like that holding that lizard?"

George said: "Yes, Mam. Just a little polly-lizard, it don't harm."

She said, pointing dramatically to the door: "Get it out of my kitchen this minute."

She said, stamping her foot, when he didn't obey her immediately: "Take it outside and kill it, next thing it will be coming inside here again."

George looked at her: "What! Kill a little no-harm polly-lizard like this?" as though he didn't dream she could really mean it.

"Take it outside and kill it, I say; this minute, you hear?"

"Ain't goin' kill it nothing," said George, defiantly, as he edged toward the door.

She brought her apron up to her eyes. "Lizards in the woodpile and all, what next!" she sighed lugubriously, looked down her nose cross-eyed.

She could hear George's whistle going away toward the woodshed. She put her hand to her mouth, made a funnel of it, called loudly: "*George!*"

"George!" she shouted, "you come right back here this minute."

George put his head in through the door.

She looked at him suspiciously: "You got rid of that lizard?"

He grinned, nodded: "I put him where he'll be happy, in the old chaff-cutter trough."

She said: "Hm!" grimly. Then, "You come in here and get every single stick of wood out of that bin, and make mighty sure there ain't no more lizards around."

She's really scared of them little polly-lizards, George thought contemptuously.

He said: "Yes, Mam," and went across to the wood bin.

She poked some of the wood he had set on the floor with her foot, then she bent down and took it in her hands. She opened the firedoor and put more wood in. She puffed out her cheeks and blew on the fire to make it blaze.

George smelled the cooking. It smelled good.

"Hm! Chicken," he said, "I can smell him frying."

"You' nose too inquisitive," she said, "you get on with what you doing."

"Yes, *Mam!*" he said, a big grin making his face come like a moon.

She backed away from the stove two paces, sighed, sat down on a stool.

George looked at her. "I know what it is," he said, "you got corns; my ole lady too. You just set down an' res' you'self, I'll cook supper fo' you."

"I could and do with a rest," she said, "been on my feet from blessed morning; same thing every day."

"All right," he said, "you jus' res' you'self now. Goin' be everything just fine an' dandy, you wait an' see."

As she sat back and watched him busy about the stove, fixing the fire, getting the wood stacked in the fireplace just right so it would burn without smoking too much, setting a damper under the pot where the chicken was frying so it wouldn't take too high a colour before it was well cooked all the way through, she sighed, loosened her corset a bit, slipped the shoes off her feet, and leaned back against the wall.

She half-closed her eyes and gazed sentimentally into the fireglow. She recollected with a kind of wistfulness that all her married life she had prayed she might have a boy.

6

Amos eased himself into a more comfortable position on the stool again. He was getting restless, He couldn't stand to see Jake all off to himself there, just sitting, brooding like that.

He said: "It's getting dark."

And Jake said: "Yes." He went on whittling at the stick, just to give his hands something to do, and it had an unnerving effect on Amos.

It was not just Jake sitting there in the gloom alone... it was himself too, he just couldn't stand it; he felt like something he had carefully built up was collapsing; he wanted to cry out in protest, to make some significant gesture to prevent what was happening... he felt thwarted and impatient, and angry and impotent. He wanted to get up and stamp about the place and rave. Only the knowledge that it would do no earthly good held him. He just had to sit and wait.

He said, tentatively, more to break the silence than anything: "Jake, you want me to light a lamp?"

"Don't you like to sit in the dark?" said Jake, with that kind of mirthless chuckle in his voice.

And Amos said: "Anything you say."

"Don't say that," said Jake sharply.

"Sorry..."

"And you don't have to be sorry about it, either. Just don't keep saying it, that's all."

"Okay, Jake... er, just like you say..."

He could have bitten his tongue off, but there it was he had said it again.

He waited for the explosion, but none came. Jake just sat with the stick and the knife in his hands, immobile, staring out through the window.

Presently Jake said, "What time is it, I wonder?"

"Must be pretty near supper time, I'm getting hungry."

And Jake said: "Ah." And then he said: "It's going to rain."

The first few spattering drops fell. They hit the roof like a shower of small pebbles.

Again that mirthless chuckle: "I told you so."

"The weather's broke, though," said Amos.

Jake didn't say anything. He just sat staring out through the window... not seeing anything before him... just staring like that.

Amos moved restlessly on the stool.

"I'll go get a lamp, eh?"

He felt the urgent need to get up and do something; if he just sat there he would scream.

He got up and limped slowly from the room.

Jake got up too, when he heard the door close softly behind Amos. He put down the knife and the stick on the table. He could find his way about easily in the dark. He moved about the room with a deftness and a sureness that gave him a sense of power, and he moved without sound.

He went across to the wall where the shotgun hung on the bracket he had made there for it. Felt, and found that the gun was still in its place.

He let his fingers run strokingly down the smooth barrel and stock. He stood like that for a long time, just feeling of the gun.

When Amos came back into the room with the lamp, Jake was sitting over by the window where he had left him. His hands rested on his knees, and he was staring out vacantly as before. It seemed to Amos as though he had never moved at all.

SIX

The rain held off. The weather had broken. Two days of sun with light showers, and the earth smiled again.

Birds sang from the wood again, and little by little it lost the dank peaty smell of sodden rotting vegetation. It smelled again sweet and fresh like the face of a young girl.

And it came around again to another quiet Sunday on the calendar, and Nature turned over on her good side this morning, and was sweet and smiling and innocent of any thought of whimsical malignancy.

Miriam remembered the bilberries that grew thick by the little spring that went winding through the wood. She took a little basket, slung it by the handle over her arm, and went walking across the common toward the wood.

George, coming in the opposite direction, saw her, hailed her: "Hi, Miriam!" And Miriam waved her hand at him, and said: "Hi!"

"Where you going this soon a-morning?"

"Going to the wood."

"Wait, I come with you."

She shook her head: "I'm going alone."

He looked at her, mischievously: "Like that, eh?" winked, "You want I should tell somebody?"

"You tell anybody I would box you, scratch you, never speak to you again." She said it quietly, standing very still, and the very stillness of her poise, the way she held herself, lent sincerity to her words.

But George was not going to give up an opportunity of teasing her so easily.

Gwan," he said, grinning at her, hard, "don't gimme that line."

"I mean it, so help me!"

"Hm! swearin' too! All right I won't tell anybody; just drop a little word in passin' like."

"George, you wouldn't. Not after what I just told you."

"You want me walk with you instead? I could hold the basket."

"I told you already I'm going alone. And if you drop a hint to – to anybody, I never speak to you long as you live, so help me!"

He saw that she meant it.

All the same...

A deep and dark plot was hatching in George's mind as he walked slowly toward the stable. He had his hands in his pockets, and he whistled tunelessly as he went. Every now and then he would stop to toss a stone in the air with his bare toes. His toes opened and closed over the stone, like fingers, and he tossed it in the air. He had been practising up that for some days past, and he was getting real good at it now.

He could hear Glen grooming down Beauty in the stable, talking to her and whistling to her, the irregular tapping of her off back hoof against the side of the stable, and Glen's occasional "Whoa there, Beauty, whoa girl; whoa!"

George came down to the stable, leaned against a railing, one foot up, chewing on a straw.

If there was one thing he meant to do, though it should be the last thing he did in life, it was to gallop Beauty on the common. Since Glen wouldn't let him, he must find a way.

He said: "Hi, Glen!"

And Glen answered him without taking his eyes off Beauty: "That you, George? Hi!"

"You going take her out this morning, Glen?"

"No."

"I'm sorry I did what I did the other day, Glen, truly."

"That's all right."

"Don't know what got in me. Must have been the devil – just give me a poke in the side, you know that way?"

But Glen didn't want to talk about it. He just grunted something, and went on grooming the mare.

George was thinking hard, and as though to disguise the thought processes going on inside him, he felt the urge to talk.

"What you doing this morning?"

"Eh?"

"Got anything special on you' mind?"

"Like what so? No, nothing. No."

He wanted George to go away, but George wouldn't take a hint. He just stood there, one-legged, chewing on the straw.

"It's Sunday, you could go to church," said George.

Glen just looked at him, his mind full of other matters, looked away again.

"Why don't you run along and play?"

"What's your idea about people going to church?"

"I got no ideas on the subject. Go on now, I'm busy."

"All right, then," said George. "I saw Miriam going to the wood just now. She asked me if I knew where you was. Just thought I would drop a hint."

Glen stopped grooming the mare, looked at George closely.

George felt perspiration pricking at the back of his neck. But he couldn't go back now, he had to go on.

"Anyway, if you don't want to talk, I guess I better get along."

Glen said, slowly: "What did she say?"

"Didn't say nothing, Glen. Just asked if I knew where you was, that's all. She was carrying one of them little baskets over her arm, so. I figured she must be going to look for bilberries down by the spring."

"Oh."

"She asked me if I knew where you was, casual like. I just thought I would drop a hint."

Beauty's off back hoof went rap-rap against the stable wall.

Glen said, quietly: "If you're lying to me, I'll take the skin off your hide."

"Awe Glen, why would I want to lie?"

The perspiration was running down the back of his neck now, tickling behind his ears.

He shrugged. "It's up to you, bwoy, you want to believe me or not. I should care, no skin off my nose!"

"All right," said Glen, "I'll just go and see. Just want to make sure you're not lying that's all."

He put up the draw-rails in front of the stable door, all his movements slow and deliberate.

George put his hands in his pockets, slouched on down the track a piece.

Glen took a short cut across the common. George turned and came back slowly toward the stable, watched him until he was lost in the wood.

He waited a few minutes more.

He was trembling a little with excitement. The blood was singing inside his ears.

He went quickly, confidently up to Beauty, she shied a little, tossed her head. He talked to her quietly, confidently, she quieted down.

He just slipped a simple rope halter over her head, brought her out of the stall, mounted her bareback, walked her down to the edge of the common.

He talked to her quietly for a while, patted her on the shoulder, until presently she stopped moving in little uneasy spurts backward and forward and sideways, and stood still in one spot, quivering like a steel coil under him.

Then he leaned forward way over her neck, and dug his heels into her flanks.

She shot forward like a stone from a slingshot, and they went for a spirited gallop across the common.

George was a born horseman; he crouched over the back of the mare like a monkey, and it seemed nothing could disturb that perfect fusion between the boy and the mare.

And it seemed Beauty too understood all about it, and exulted and thrilled to that gallop, as she had never done before.

And so they exulted together in that gallop across the common, and at last George pulled her down to a gentle ambling gait, and so to a walk. And he rode her like that, slap back inside the stable, and she never even remembered to balk at the door.

He gave her a brisk rub down, patting her lovingly, and talking to her all the time. And when he was finished he put back the draw-rails in their place.

Beauty turned around in her stall, and put her head over the top draw-rail, and whinnied to him as he went down the track. He turned and kissed his hands to her. He was grinning all over his face.

He went on a little further, and then he suddenly remembered about something. His hand went inside, the front of his shirt, and he took out the *guzung-fet*. He looked at it reverently for a moment, kissed it, put it back inside his shirt.

"*Guzung-fet*," he said, his voice low and fervent with prayer, "you better work for me hard."

2

She had gathered all the best bilberries just across the spring, but she noticed the biggest clusters grew higher up. All she had to do was to clamber over a boulder to get to them. Her dress got in her way.

She put the basket down, pulled some withes, tucked her skirt way up, and secured it with the green withes about her waist.

She looked down at her bare legs and laughed.

Then she kicked off her shoes, and started to climb the damp, slippery boulder to get at the berries beyond.

She was straddled across the boulder, half way up it, holding on with one hand to a green switch which had rooted itself firmly in a crack in the rock, the other clutching at a crumbly spur of rotting limestone, when she heard the loud cracking of a dry stick behind her.

She stopped trying to pull herself up across the slippery rock face, threw a glance over her shoulder, suddenly let go, giving up all she had gained thereby, came lightly to her feet, turned and faced him. There was something in her gesture of turning at bay.

Glen stood looking at her across the narrow trickle of water. Her eyes were angry, challenging, curious, questioning, all together like that, looking back at him.

He stood like a man whose intention had suddenly become cancelled out inside him, just staring at her in a foolish sort of way.

Her eyes gathered fury, and went cold again, and she said, in a voice that sounded strangely breathless and held-in.

"Why you come here?"

"I – " he broke off. "I came for a walk. I remembered about the bilberries too."

She didn't say anything. She leaned against the boulder, and her quiet, still gaze challenged him, as though it meant to say "So now why don't you go away?"

Deep down inside her, her anger still smouldered... she couldn't think clearly what it was made her so angry, but it swept through her with a sense of righteous indignation, and it was as though by his very presence there he had violated something that was her own right.

She said, now: "I got here first."

And if she didn't actually see him wince, it was because he was holding himself in. And she knew it.

"Did – did anybody send you?"

It was another taunt.

He wanted to turn and go back without a word, but something held him; something that was stronger than his will held him still, with everything cancelled out inside him like that.

He shook his head. "No."

It seemed as though a spasm of relief flitted across her face, but her eyes were cold, and hot, and challenging, the same.

He was standing right beside a tall, straight sapling, the leaves of which had a strange, pungent odour, when he took and crushed them in his hands.

The wind came, and bent the sapling over, so that it rubbed against his shoulder, and drew away.

He put out his hand, and took one of the slender, switchlike branches, about the thickness of his finger. He broke it off suddenly, without thinking about it, and started stripping it of its leaves.

Her eyes burned suddenly, hotly, an instant, looking at him.

He went on stripping the leaves, crushing them between his fingers, felt a strange, voluptuous sensation going up his arms.

She laughed three short, bright notes: deliberately turned her back to him, started climbing the boulder, acting as though he wasn't there.

She was straddled half way up it, when the rotting jut of stone gave under her fingers. With a cry of surprise and dismay she came tumbling down again.

Something raked her leg. It started to bleed. She was a little shaken, from her fall.

She looked up from staring mutely at the blood on her thigh, saw him standing there beside her.

"Miriam! You hurt yourself?"

He was lifting her in his arms.

She laughed a little jerkily, his sudden movement had unnerved her. She laughed, with her head back against his shoulder. He kissed her on the mouth.

She said, still laughing like that: "I – I thought you were going to beat me!"

And he answered her quickly, earnestly: "Don't ever say a thing like that!"

3

Bess was out in the back yard in a patch of sunlight washing out some dishcloths, and she was singing with a deal of lush emotion in her thick, throaty voice. She sang *Sweet Little Jesus Boy*, because she was filled with a great sense of release and happiness. And she sang and sang, until presently she was swept up and carried away with the emotion she had generated, and tears came to her eyes.

She had stood the tub on an upturned iron drum that had been cut in two, and now she hefted the tub to the ground, and sat on the iron drum herself, and took her apron in her hands and brought it up to her eyes. She just let herself go, and had a good cry. And all because she was so happy, and life seemed so good this day.

After she had had her cry out she felt weak and hungry, so she went inside the kitchen and got herself a snack, and she came outside and sat her down on the iron drum again and ate it; a good cry always made her feel hungry, that was a fact.

She didn't see when Jake left the house, through the back door.

He closed the back door quietly behind him, and headed straight for the wood. He was carrying a shotgun in his hand. He walked quickly, and with a firm step, full of decision.

He had little difficulty picking his way toward the familiar track, because the underbrush did not grow thick between the trees at the edge of the wood.

Little by little his feet renewed their acquaintance with the old familiar path.

He walked along briskly, and then stopped. He leaned his ear to one side, listening.

He walked along a bit again. And stopped.

And then suddenly he stepped off the path.

He stood close against a tall cottonwood tree, holding himself straight and close against it. And then he deliberately made a little sound, treading some brambles under his feet, and waited.

Amos was limping past the cottonwood tree, close enough to it, and Jake moved quickly, guided only by the sound he made, he just put out an arm and touched Amos, and Amos let out a short, startled cry, and Jake's forearm slipped around from behind and under his throat.

Amos put both hands up to his forearm and struggled with all his strength to break that stranglehold. And Jake had to lift him clear off his feet and hold him like that against him, to make him quit struggling.

"Steady now, old timer," said Jake, close against his ear, and Amos gave a kind of jerk with his head.

"Take it easy now," said Jake, setting him down on his feet again, and relaxing his hold a little, "else I'll be hurting you, maybe, without meaning to."

"Let me go," said Amos.

"That's better," said Jake, and he loosed his arm from about Amos. "Now tell me, what are you doing out here at this time. You know you got no business out here in the wood, you were down the field working."

"I was, but I got tired of that," Amos said, gruffly, "and I come out here for a walk, same as you."

"Would it be that you are following me? Don't you know there are times when a man wants to be alone?"

"All right," said Amos, "so you want to be alone. So then you sneak off out here, through the back door – just because you want to be alone. And I've no bloody business following you."

"Hush, man! Don't swear."

"All right. All right. But suppose – just suppose I got the feeling I wanted to sneak off on my own, too. And suppose I should decide to take this track through the wood, just the same as you – "

Jake said: "All right, let's suppose it – all the things you've thought up with your cussed cleverness. But I got here first, didn't I?"

"I guess you're right." And after a moment. "Look here, Jake, supposing we strike a bargain."

"Let's hear it."

"Give me your word you won't do anything – anything mad like –" Amos was breathing with difficulty, "that you – or someone else – won't be sorry for, after. Promise me that, and I won't follow you another step."

A silence seemed to shuttle through the wood. It wove itself about them.

Then Jake said, slowly: "I promise you, old timer, I won't do anything that anybody should be sorry for."

The silence went on about them, as though everything stood still.

Amos said: "I guess I'll just have to take that." He seemed to have difficulty with his breathing. "Goodbye, Jake."

"You going back to the house now?"

"I said I wasn't going to follow you. Ain't that enough?"

"Yes, I guess that's fair enough."

Jake turned and went off slowly down the track.

Amos stood and watched him go, until he was lost among the trees. And the silence moved over, and the wind went shaking through the wood.

And presently a woman walked toward him, from over the other side of the track. Amos only looked up when she stood directly in front of him.

He said, dully: "What are you doing here?"

"The same thing as you. I have a right to come here if I wish. I am still his wife."

He said, without bitterness, anything: "You! Don't make me laugh."

"I know. I know how you feel about me…"

Only his eyes showed his contempt. His words still came from him flat and dry as a shingle. "That's fine."

"I come here often," the woman said, "when it's fair. You used to come here often yourself – to be alone."

He said, his voice thick with sarcasm: "It's a nice morning to come a walk in the wood."

But she went on, as though she didn't notice anything: "It's not too far from where I live. I'm working now. I've got a job. Social welfare work."

"Look here, what do you want?"

"I don't know," she said. "Do you?" And then she said, "I just want to talk, maybe. Just – talk to someone – "

"I don't want no talk with you."

"You might, for all I know, it's about him I want to talk."

"Jake?"

"Yes… I guessed that would hold you. You love him…"

"Mind your own business."

"It's my business, too, I'm his wife – and *I* love him."

"Don't make me laugh… but you went off with another man."

"Yes. And if you want to know I did that *because* I love him."

"Who? Not Jake."

"Anyway, that's not what I want to talk about."

"Oh!"

"I know you hate me. I don't blame you, either."

"That's nice of you. It makes me proud to hear it."

She drew a long, slow breath, and let it go again. "The biggest and finest thing he ever did, is what he has done for you… you know that. I don't blame you for hating me; for being loyal to him. You are living proof that he really was as big and good, underneath, as I always thought him."

"Was?"

"All right. Don't let us wrangle over words. You know what I mean."

"Go on."

"You've grown into somebody, Amos. You will never go back to being nobody again. Jake's done that for you. No wonder you're proud to be his friend."

"All right, we'll leave that out, and get on with the rest. What are you getting at, anyway?"

"But he could never forgive you that he had to be dependent upon you for something. It's in him. He just can't help it."

"What are you talking about?"

"I'm talking about Jake. We got on fine, until he found out that he was leaning on me too much…"

"You! You don't think a hell of a lot of yourself, do you?"

She said, quietly: "I know what I am talking about. He knew it, and he hated to know it. For a time he tried to close his eyes to it… it was bound to destroy him." She said, after a moment's hesitation: "Why didn't he ever finish that carving?"

"Don't you know?"

"It's not his blindness, if that's what you mean."

"You were a schoolteacher before he married you, you always thought yourself a cut above him."

She went on, as though she didn't hear him:

"It was while he was trying to finish his carving that he found out."

"What do you know about it?"

"And then for months he stopped working on it… and life with him became unbearable. I couldn't tell anyone what I went through in those months… he and I, both."

"You're not one for being sorry for yourself, are you?"

"Until at last I saw there was nothing for it but for me to go away."

"And I suppose you didn't love the other man at all!"

"You can leave that out of it – for the present – it can only cloud the issue."

"Yes?"

"I'm not trying to make up excuses for myself. Why should I want to make excuses for my actions to you?"

"Why you want to talk to me about it, at all?"

"For other reasons altogether, and you know it."

"All right. I guess I just don't understand what you are trying to say… or why you're trying to say it."

"You want to know the truth? He – he couldn't finish it without – without help from outside. And he knew it. And it made him hate me."

"You are lying; and I shouldn't even be listening to you."

Her voice became hard. "He lived by people's adulation, without even knowing it. Without it he was lost, and there was – nothing."

"You bitch!"

"But he also helped you to find yourself. That's something."

"Oh, forget it. I shouldn't even be listening to you."

"Some day you'll understand what I'm trying to say."

He said, doggedly, getting his teeth into something that he understood: "Jake is my friend."

She looked at him, and her eyes said nothing: "I know it."

She said: "Do you think I'm asking you to be disloyal to your friend? It's not that at all. Someday you'll know."

"All right, suppose we wait until then?"

She looked at him, and her eyes lit with reluctant admiration now: "You've got the right stuff in you. The stuff that human friendship is made of, I won't say another word."

He said, after a longish pause: "So you think he ducked out from under things; that's what you're trying to say, eh? I suppose you believe that he even arranged it so that that stroke of lightning should blind him for the rest of his life just so that people could be sorry for him."

"I believe we shape the circumstances that make us what we are – in the end. I can't explain it better, but I know what I mean."

"You do think so then! You sure mean proud by him!"

"We're talking about two different things."

"So he made that lightning strike him... look, you make me want to vomit – if you'll excuse me."

"You're missing the point... you're not being fair to him..."

"Who? Me?"

"All right. I won't say anything..."

"You're full of words..."

"And they say the wrong things – they twist the things I want to say."

"Christ!"

"I know – I know... we can't do anything about it."

"Oh Jesus Christ! God damn it!"

"Hush!"

"Let me be. I got to say it… with – with him out there, even now… with the thought of death in his heart – "

"I know."

She bowed her head until her chin was resting on her bosom. She was weeping, without making any sound.

He looked at her, and said, suddenly, with a kind of break in his voice: "Don't do that."

She lifted her face and looked at him, shook her head, with the tears streaming down her cheeks. "No. No. It is all right." Her words came rapidly, as though she was afraid something might happen to her, and she wouldn't get to the end of them. "You couldn't turn him aside. You must know that for yourself. If you tried to argue with him… would only make it worse. Perhaps – perhaps if you hadn't followed him here, there's a chance he might have changed his mind even…"

He was shocked with the sudden realization. "Good God!"

"What have I said? Don't mind anything I say. I'm taking it hard."

"It's not true! You don't believe that?"

"No! No!" She shook her head in violent denial. "No, it isn't true. I'm talking wild."

He said, hating her, "You hate him; and you would say anything!" taking comfort from the thought.

It was as though his own salvation lay in his accusation of her; and he knew it.

She didn't seem to hear him; she said, holding herself in: "It's a pity we can't be friends, you and me."

He said, hating her more than ever: "You want for us to be friends! Don't make me laugh!"

"Maybe you'll understand what I'm saying yet."

"You wouldn't kid yourself, would you? Oh you bitch, you bitch!"

He had the need deep down to channel his emotions into something, and hating her with all his heart was it.

She said: "I have got to go now. But perhaps we'll meet again – soon."

"Yes.'

"Why did you let him go off alone with the gun?"

"What could I do?" And then his anger making him violent: "It's his business what he wants to do, isn't it?"

"And yours, and mine – when it comes to that." For she too must have a stick to beat him with. She, too, with things coming up inside her, that were too, too much.

That put him on the defensive again, and it was what she wanted. "All right; but you can't force a man to go on living, just because *you* want him to."

"Well, that's what I expected you to say…"

"You bitch!"

"Don't call me that again."

"Why?"

"Because it's cowardly. It isn't true."

He quailed before her, suddenly, because of some quality that was in her, that made him ashamed.

"All the same, if you hadn't let him down…"

"Don't you believe it. Let's give him his due; don't rob him of any part of it by pretending about anything."

"Do you realize that while we're here talking…"

"Yes. Yes."

Looking about him suddenly: "How peaceful it is in the wood… everywhere – Estella!"

"Yes?"

"Well, ain't it – curious!"

"Yes. Is that what you want me to say?"

Suddenly.

"Estella! Don't go yet… for a while. I don't want you should go."

"Yes."

"I guess – I guess you got – a right to be here."

"Yes."

She said: "I knew you would see it, too."

"You are always right. I guess you've always had heaps more sense than the rest of us."

"Don't you believe it. I've made a muddle of everything. I could have done a heap better."

He suddenly went up to her, and held her hand.

They stood like that, as though suspended in time, waiting for the end of the world.

4

They came at last to rest on a fallen log in a clearing. He made her sit down, and he set down the basket of berries beside her on the grass, and he sat beside her on the log.

"How is the leg, is it painful?"

"I 'most forgot about it already."

He looked around him, loving every bit of it.

The pea-doves called plaintively to each other under the sweetwood trees. The trees let down their branches and all came to a hush in the wood, that was broken only, occasionally, by the distant cooing of the wild pea-doves. The whole was informed throughout with a sense of peace.

He reached for her hand, opened it palm upward, traced with his finger the line of the heart, and closed her fist tightly about it.

He said: "It's like the furthest place we could go to be away from the rest of the world."

"The wood is so full of peace... If I had to die, I think I would like to die out here."

His arm tightened about her waist.

"Don't talk about dying. We want to live. Ain't it?"

"Yes, Glen. We want to live... for a long, long time..."

"That's the way to talk, girl, that's the stuff."

A little wind came, and lifted the branches of the trees, and went with a sound like the rustle of silk through the tall grass. And the tall trees stood still again, as though they had never moved at all; as though they were possessed of a secret that awed them to silence. The shadows huddled in their dark blue coats like a host in ambush under the still trees.

She leaned against his shoulder, half-closed her eyes, murmured sleepily: "Say something."

"September just round the corner. The birds are flying over to find new feeding-grounds in the hills."

"I know. The whitewings and the baldpates."

"And the ringtails and the pea-doves."

"Soon they'll be shooting at them. You too – I hate the thought... just now."

"Silly! It's good sport."

"I know. Still and all…"

A single gunshot shattered the silence of the wood.

She sat up suddenly, clutched his arm.

"What is that!"

He said, trying to calm her fears: "It's nothing. Someone getting in his first crack at the birds."

He drew her back into the protective circle of his arm.

A shudder shook through her.

"It frightened me. I'm gooseflesh all over." She shivered again.

"Why you shiver like that? You cold?"

"No. I dunno," she answered slowly. "Must be something walked over my grave."

BLACK LIGHTNING – AN AFTERWORD

JEREMY POYNTING

"But it was like a man speaking a parable, it sounded many notes together in the hearer's mind" (p. 59).

"It was something else again that went about the world wanting a name, and men called it this or that, but it meant more and other, and was without a name" (p. 111).

Jacqueline Bishop's introduction to *Black Lightning* offers a lovely invitation to read that suggests the range of the novel's concerns, including the love story between Amos and Jake. She writes of the story as being hidden from a society not ready for it, and that is true. I want to go back to that one element in more detail – to look at the formal strategies Mais uses to smuggle more into this narrative than appears on the surface, and, because this aspect of the novel has mostly been ignored, to say a little more about it.

Of all Mais's novels this is the most carefully and densely structured, and within its apparently conventional form I think Mais questions, in a remarkable way, the capacity of language to express the world. He does this by creating a tension between precision of expression and the use of a deliberate inarticulacy in many of his characters' exchanges. This emphasis on what is unsayable works in both metonymic and metaphoric ways. It is at the root of the difficulties and failures in his characters' relationships, but it also suggests a world that is more various – in culture, sexuality, and morals – than the rule-makers in the novel, and in the Jamaican society in which *Black Lightning* is set, would wish it to be.

The novel smuggles in its exploration of a homosexual love story by strategies of parallelisms, displacements, verbal echoes, recurring symbolic objects (including an axe, accordion, wasp, carving and gun), leakages, subtle contrasts, allusions and quite deliberate vaguenesses of expression to create densely woven connections between the relationships of Jake and Amos, Miriam and Glen and George and Beauty. What Mais is able to say directly about Miriam and Glen, and metaphorically about George and Beauty, can be read as proxy ways of addressing what he can't say directly about Jake and Amos. For instance, the sexual metaphors that Mais uses (perhaps to excess) in describing the easy relationship between boy and horse comment directly on the mess Glen and Miriam are making of their courtship, but they can also be read as speaking about what is deeply repressed between Jake and Amos.

Their relationship is also embedded in the overarching, connecting motifs that give the novel its organic unity. These include the opposition between the impulses to power and control and the equality of giving, between suspicions of the body and delight in it, and between repressiveness and tolerance in communities. There is, for instance, something Blakean in the contrasts Mais draws between Glen's urge to control Miriam, Jake's inability to accept that he can't dominate Amos, and George's rule-breaking enjoyment in riding Beauty. As Blake warns: "He who binds to himself a joy/ Does the winged life destroy/ But he who kisses the joy as it flies/ Lives in eternity's sun rise".[1]

One of the devices Mais foregrounds early in the novel, as both a connective narrative strategy and as a recurring focus on his characters' capacity for self-deception, is displacement. When Glen quite unjustly gives George a painful belting, he realises, of course, "that it was not George he wanted to give a good belting to, but Miriam" (p. 47). This episode is immediately followed by a conversation between Jake and Amos, where their discomfort with their increasing intimacy is displaced onto talk about the weather (pp. 48-50), and Jake's verbal snapping at Amos echoes Glen's belting of George ("And Amos just sat back, cowed, as though he [Jake] had struck him across the face" (p. 50). The scene ends, though, with Jake asking Amos to stay the night – because of the weather!

As Jacqueline Bishop notes, another strategy Mais employs is deliberate vagueness. There are many places where he invites the reader to ask, "But what is this character really saying?" After one of Jake's and Amos's circular, evasive dialogues there is an authorial comment – "But it was like a man speaking a parable, it sounded many notes together in the hearer's mind" (p. 59) – that could stand as an epigraph for the novel. It is there when Miriam and Glen are discussing Jake and she says, "You wouldn't be jealous of Jake" and he asks "Is he so different from other men?" and she responds "… oh, but you *couldn't* be jealous of him…" (p. 20), which of course poses the question: Why not? Later, Glen's observations about Jake hint at something more than just the bitterness of a cuckolded man (which is how you would expect Glen to see him): "the difference wasn't something you could just put your finger on and say it is this or it is that; it was *something other, and more*" [my italics] (p. 43). And look at how we are invited to read the quarrel between Bess and Amos when they are arguing about their respective rights to be in the wood. Amos says, "The wood ain't mine more than it is yours, all the same a man has a right to be alone, who come so far to find it." So why does Bess choose to question what "it" might be? But she does:

"Find what?" […]
"Never mind what. If I was to tell you you wouldn't understand." (p. 28)

On the contrary, Bess would understand. From the start she suspects that there is something deeper in the relationship, and later it is her household that models a community of tolerance.

As Jacqueline Bishop notes, Mais complicates the significance of Jake's preoccupation with the Samson story, and she reads it as a welcome revision of the maligned figure of Delilah – which it clearly is – but it can also be read as Jake's vehicle for thinking about his sexuality. On the surface, it appears to be about his "betrayal" by Estella, but Jake's attraction to the story predates Estella's departure. He is described as "thinking over the causes and issues of his life and what must have gone on under the surface between himself [sic] and Delilah. Things that the Bible never mentioned at all. Things other than, and more complex, and in a way more disturbing than what was discovered in the bald account" (p. 52). Again, Mais invites the reader to wonder what these things could be. Jake considers how Delilah was attracted by

Samson's "great strength, his virility. But he had not lost that", and wonders if Delilah was in love "with one of her own people" (a further displacement?). However, as an explanation it clearly does not satisfy him – on the evidence of the sledgehammer thrown through the wall. (p. 50)

By the time we first see Jake and Amos together, Mais has already put in place a number of narrative devices which frame their dialogue – the expectation of leakages and echoes between episodes, the themes of power and the absence of self-knowledge, and the very deliberate use of evasiveness in their dialogue:

> "You know somep'n, Jake," he said and broke off suddenly.
> [...] "Well what's it?" he said. "What you got on your mind, pardner?"
> "Oh, nothing, Jake."
> "Must be something, pardner, you can tell me."
> "I forget." (p. 34)

At this point, though Jake seems innocent of the implications of their relationship, Amos appears to have some awareness of the kind of man he is. While Jake talks about men and women, Amos speaks about "how *people* come together in the world and do things between them like" (p. 36). But if at this stage Amos has a greater awareness of his feelings, he is also evidently conflicted about them. As he plays his accordion the images that "leapt abruptly to the forefront of his mind" are of heaven and hell: "golden harps" and "others, ugly ones" (p. 62). There is, too, the episode when Amos accidentally maims a bird, and then kills and buries it. We are told, "It was his secret. And nobody would ever know what lay hidden under that stone". However, as he walks away, Mais adds, "his fear walked with him always at his shoulder" (p. 63). What does he fear? We are not told, but the very next episode shows community intolerance in action. Whilst none of those who come name the problem as the relationship between the two men (Mother Coby complains of Jake's sacrilege in making a graven image (p. 63), and Tata Joe and Massa Butty tell Jake he is wasting his education (pp. 78-82)), there are enough clues to suggest the real reason. There is the old men's embarrassed laughter and Massa Butty's body language as he "leaned forward slightly, fixed him with his gaze./ "You think it's right you should be doing this?" (p. 79)

Pressed, Massa Butty opts for the least offensive definition of "this" – Jake's work as a blacksmith, when he could be doing more elevated things, though the occupation he suggests (public works foreman) is really no higher status. We get nearer the truth when Massa Butty blurts out: "Why don't you go away, Jake" (p. 80), and Tata Joe says, when Jake is absent, "Beats me how he stands that muggin, Amos, around him all the time like that" (p. 82).

Jacqueline Bishop rightly discusses the carving in terms of religious puritanism and the vexed relationship of the artist to the community, but it can also be read as concerning Jake's discovery of a self he is unable, ultimately, to accept. This is suggested when Miriam witnesses Jake's crisis of confidence – his "wanting of vision, a blindness, a blur…", the trembling hesitancy, and thinks "oh God, he has done something wrong" (p. 68). But when Jake's vision clears and he sees "the coming into being of something, the image of which was locked into his mind", *what* this is has to be deduced by the reader. The location of the *what* is suggested when Miriam asks Jake about what is on *her* mind – her relationship with Glen – and Jake responds with fury: "Love? Ha! Look at *him*!" […] "Ask him what does *he* think of love (p. 69)" – he being the carved head. Now, this might be taken as a reference to Estella and Jake's sense of betrayal, but his earlier rejection of conventional readings of the Samson and Delilah story hints that his confusions about love may lie elsewhere. That elsewhere is suggested in Jake's discomfort with his growing intimacy with Amos, though it is Jake who opens the declarations: "We are a couple of queer ones, eh pardner? You and me. I guess that's why we get along together. To most people you're poison, but to me…"[…] "It's just like we're kin." [And we cannot think that Mais, who spent several years in London in the early 1950s, would not have known the meaning of queer as homosexual, though there is no evidence of the word being used in that way in Jamaica]. A "thoughtful" Amos echoes the term: "Just a couple of God's creatures born out in the cold. You an' me. Kin. That's us." Jake's response ("Don't know much about us being born that way, pardner. Maybe we did that ourselves" (p. 74)) goes to the heart of his perplexity about himself and the difference in self-knowledge between himself and Amos. If Amos moves towards self-acceptance, Jake never really loses his anxiety about being in a state of disobedience – as his embarrassed: "For Christ sake… let's talk about something else" suggests.

With Amos, Jake is unable to speak about what the carving means: "Oh it's coming along" […] It's – there's something…"/ "Well?"/"Oh, forget it" (p. 60). Then in the scene leading to his blinding, when he takes Amos to see the carving for the first time, Jake expresses his fear that something cataclysmic is happening, that "the world underneath us, holding us up … going out like a spark in darkness" (p. 85)). Jake's explanation of the carving – of the blinded, vulnerable Samson – is both universal and deeply personal:

> "Look, Amos, if you could gather up all the suffering there is in the world… of all the folks who had lost their way in some kind of darkness, and of all who have known *any kind of lack that human flesh and spirit can know* […] you would get something like that…" (p. 87) [my emphasis].

Jake also makes a less explicit but perhaps even more fundamental connection between himself and the carving when he asks: "Where will he take that burden to its last resting-place, and set it down? *And be restored to himself, whole*? [my italics]" (p. 87). Now, I am not saying that even this strand of the novel is solely about thwarted queer desires because this is just one element in Mais's existential perception of human suffering and the tragic fate of the conscious person in a godless, absurd ("crazy", p. 88) world. But the pertinence of Jake's "any kind of lack that human flesh and spirit can know" to his feelings about Amos is suggested in the physicality of his attempt to prevent Amos from leaving the loft when he "held him pinned to his side, struggling with all his strength" (p. 88). Later, Amos is clear about the meaning of the carving for their relationship; when Jake chops up the head he recognises it as a symbolic act of self-rejection, foretelling his suicide.

But Jake cannot evade reflection on "why it was that he encouraged the ugly little hunchback about him", or on how "In a way he liked Amos and sometimes hated him… there were things about him he hated worse than poison." When he finds another Biblical narrative to describe his request that Amos play his accordion to him (David, in the Book of Samuel, playing before Saul to soothe the evil spirit that has been put upon him), he doesn't see the tragic irony that it is what he feels for Amos that is the problem. This is how we might read the evasiveness of what follows: "So that was it after all, he encouraged Amos not for Amos' sake, but because of the good he got out of it. *And then another thought came and put this one out of his mind*" [my emphasis] (p. 58). The nearest Jake comes to an admission of physical feeling is the image of how "he wanted to overlay the other's weakness with his own strength, as a man might put his own coat about another to shield him from the cold" (p. 58). It is an image that is both intimate *and* evasive of the physical, an image produced by a man who "felt uncomfortable, thinking about himself and Amos".

If one barrier to the enjoyment of desire is the impulse to control it, as an expression of power, the other is the destructiveness of sexual shame, a theme prefigured in the scene where Bess feeds Jake an apple pie in which a wasp has secreted itself. It is a version of Blake's worm in the rose, the snake in Eden: "O Rose thou art sick./The invisible worm,/That flies in the night/ In the howling storm://Has found out thy bed/ Of crimson joy:/And his dark secret love/ Does thy life destroy."[2] Serio-comic the wasp might be, but reading it as a symbolic representation of the destructiveness of sexual shame does not seem misplaced.

After his blinding, Jake returns to the subject of the carving as a way of talking about the source and legitimacy of his feelings: "You believe, Amos, that something a man is creating out of himself like can – take itself a soul of its own, so to speak – with ideas of its own, that you can never put there?" In the face of Amos's incomprehension he continues: "And at last it takes its own end into its own hands, in a manner of speaking, and becomes what it wants to be, declaring its own form and meaning, that wasn't in the man…" What Jake's monologue drives at, I think, is his anxiety over whether he is the product of God's making, or is in disobedience to that making: ("Does he create him down to the last atom and pulse of life and intelligence and will that's inside him?" (p. 95)), or whether he is free to chose his own identity.

The centrality of this theme to the novel is made even clearer in the next chapter (2/9) where Amos and Miriam meet in the woods, both seeking escape from the oppressive atmosphere of the house. Miriam has "a sudden, impulsive warming toward him, she felt she could lay bare her heart to this stranger, who was not a stranger any more" (p. 113). Indeed, what she sees in Amos (and Amos sees in her) is a mirror image. Her question is, of course, about whether she should follow her desires ("If a girl should be in love with a young man…" p. 114), but when Amos looks into her face and sees her looking "so wistful and lost […] something seemed to stir deep down inside him, moved *like an unseen hand putting aside the curtains in a dark room*… […] He could guess what was going on in her mind. Suddenly it announced itself in his own consciousness, *as though he had heard an imperative knocking at the gate of the house next door*. […] It stirred him strangely, making him acutely self-conscious all at once" (pp. 113-114) [my italics]. Could Mais have been any more explicit within the obliqueness he accepts as necessary for this novel? Further, when Miriam avoids saying directly what she means ("should she let him do things to her? […] You know that way"), I don't think Amos's deeply considered "Yes" is for her alone. This is evident when he says, and then tries to unsay, what is evidently not a thought about Miriam:

> "It will never be the same again…"
> "Eh? What you said?"
> "Oh, nothing."
> "You said it will never be the same again. What you mean by that?"
> "I said that?"
> "Yes, you did. What does it mean."
> "It can mean about anything, I guess." (p. 115)

It is by such indirections that Mais speaks parables about queer desire. What Amos feels is revealed when he turns to his accordion and plays a lovesong to the world, and to himself ("What a lovely miracle of a night with wind and moon… Amos, you amount to something now… And nothing will ever be the same again" (p. 116)). All this he connects closely to Jake, ("Even Jake knows that, even Jake lonely in his darkness in the big house") though the multiple meanings of "in his darkness" warns of what is to follow. When Amos returns to the house, Jake is welcoming but restless; he detects some change in Amos which Amos describes evasively as "feeling good, that's all" (p. 117). What is clear is that Jake cannot cope with the new Amos because he sees the relationship in terms of power, and fears that the power relations have shifted. He tries to belittle Amos by reminding him of his terror of lightning ("Jake laughed. It wasn't a good laugh"), but it is clear that it is now Jake who is frightened (his hand is shaking) and after more evasive dialogue, when the crash of thunder comes, it is Jake who begs Amos to come to him:

> "Amos!" he said. And, louder, higher: "Amos!" again.
> And Amos sprang up and limped across to him.
> "Here I am, Jake."
> "Don't touch me! Take your hands off. I'll smash you, Amos. You hear." (p. 118)

What can this be other than the expression of desire and the repression of desire? It leaves Jake trembling, confused, ashamed ("God, Amos! I – I could have smashed you"). Crying, he is led inside, held roughly by the shoulder (to disguise the real tenderness of his feelings) by Amos. It is at this moment that Jake comes closest to Amos; thereafter he withdraws.

As Jacqueline Bishop indicates, Estella's voice is really important in the novel. She is the most self-aware, most articulate of all the characters, and, as such, perhaps the most reliable commentator on the behaviour of others. There's her calm response to Glen's misogyny, the look that makes him feel "abashed, ashamed [...] a fool, brash and stupid, and out of his depth" (p. 122). Estella is most clearly Mais's voice in the novel, pinpointing some of its themes, not least on the subject of "rights" – including rights to sexual identity and love exchanged without coercive control – when she says self-critically, "What are rights to people like us – you and me? [...] We don't have any rights, like that... we have only symptoms of possessiveness [...] and "fits of petulance, when we have lost". She makes an honest admission that covers many of the characters, but one that insists that we take her claim to have left Jake because "I wanted us both to have a chance" (p. 123) as the truth. What she doesn't say is exactly what "his chance" means. Perhaps she's saying that she and Jake have rights as sexual beings, and though she loves him, they cannot enjoy these rights together. This theme of rights and possession is replayed in the dialogue between Amos and Bess when they talk about yet another stand-off between Glen and Miriam, and Bess says, "If she knew what I knew at her age, she'd be well and able to hold her man…" and Amos replies, "Perhaps she doesn't want to hold him. Maybe she got other ideas" (p. 127). Bess returns the comment by suggesting that Amos should perhaps question his own exclusiveness in only caring for Jake, telling him "You've got to let yourself go among people". When Bess finally "outs" him: "She looked at him closely. 'You love him, don't you?'" (p. 130), Amos's response ("He didn't reply, just sat scowling at her across the table") shows that he knows she doesn't just mean "very good friend" – though this is how he explains it: "he's been a powerful good friend to me". Bess doesn't let him get away with this, and Amos acknowledges that: "He's given me my life again, *as a man*. Do you understand what I mean? Now I have something. I have him now, to lean on me" (p. 130) [my emphasis]. And we can note the significant difference between Jake's former insistence that as the possessor of power in the relationship he will protect Amos, and Amos's mutually respectful offer of a shoulder to lean on. But how is one supposed to read his next admission to Bess, delivered in "scarcely above a whisper":

> "I used to think how folks would stop and stare. And maybe they would say 'howdy' to me, passing in the street… folks would stop me in the street and speak to me. They would want to shake my hand." (p. 130)

He says no more because he is interrupted by Jake's entry into the room, but the subjunctive tense suggests he is not talking just about his physical disability (actually no more than a limp), but some future possibility of community acceptance. I think we are meant to see Amos's physical state in a metaphorical way, that his real difference lies elsewhere.

But if Amos has remade himself by accepting who he is – a man who loves another man – Jake's path heads inexorably towards his suicide. It starts with his withdrawal from being read to, from his art, but above all from close engagement with Amos. In part this reflects his inability to accept that he and Amos can relate as equals. He sees the new Amos as occupying the dominant position he once had, and cannot see that Amos is not behaving as he himself one did. He sees Amos as "treating me like a child now", whereas the truth is that Amos is constantly fearful of saying the wrong thing.

None of this approach to *Black Lightning* makes any assumptions about Roger Mais's personal biography. Curiosity is idle; the novel's multilayered power is what is important, but one wonders. Is Jake's blindness a punishment for his impiety, as Mother Coby claims, where the making of a graven image stands for a breach of the sexual order, or is it a symbolic blindness that represents Jake's inability to see, to accept who he truly is?

It might seem that Mais indicts Jamaica for its inability to find space for Jake and Amos. I think his view is more balanced than that. Clearly Mother Coby, Massa Butty and Tata Joe and in part Glen represent a Protestant Jamaica of "Thou Shalt Not", but who is more Jamaican that Bess and George? The former creates a community of tolerance in the house where she cooks for Jake and Amos, and the latter, the free-spirited, puckish boy, who kisses joy as it flies, who significantly is the only character who speaks in Jamaican patois throughout, signals his allegiance to a much older Jamaican spiritual tradition, relatively uncontaminated by colonialism, with that other graven image, his guzung-fet.

1. William Blake, "Eternity", *Miscellaneous Poems and Fragments*, *Blake Complete Poetry and Prose*, Ed. Geoffrey Keynes (London: Nonesuch, 1961), p. 99.
2. William Blake, "The Sick Rose", *Songs of Experience*, *Blake Complete Poetry and Prose*, p. 71.

ABOUT THE AUTHOR

Roger Mais was born into a middle-class Jamaican family, spending his boyhood in the Blue Mountains, where his father took up farming. At home, he received a thorough grounding in the Bible, whose language and cadences are heard in his work. He entered Calabar High School in Kingston. From the age of seventeen to his thirties, he earned his living in a variety of jobs: office work, selling insurance, overseer on a banana plantation and as a reporter-photographer and a variety of other journalistic occupations.

In the early 1930s Mais began writing verse and short stories, and later a number of plays. He was swept up in the riots and workers' rebellion of 1938, and thereafter was a wholly committed supporter and activist involved with the PNP and Jamaican nationalism. His essays and short stories, mostly published in *Public Opinion*, were the literary adjunct to Edna Manley's discovery of an insurgent anti-colonial Jamaican spirit in sculpture.

He published two collections of stories, *Face and Other Stories*, and *And Most of All Man* in 1942. He began painting around this time. His critique of Churchill's imperialist ideology, "Now We Know", brought Mais to court and he was sentenced to six months in prison for sedition. His experience fed into his first published novel. He wrote further unpublished novels and plays before finding a publisher for *The Hills Were Joyful Together* in 1951, followed by *Brother Man* in 1954 and *Black Lightning* in 1955.

He left Jamaica for the UK in 1952, but whilst in France in 1954 discovered that he had terminal cancer. He returned to Jamaica, attempted to finish a fourth novel, but died before its completion in 1955.

CARIBBEAN MODERN CLASSICS

Now in print

Wayne Brown, *On The Coast*
ISBN 9781845231507, pp. 115, £8.99
Introduction: Mervyn Morris

George Campbell, *First Poems*
ISBN: 9781845231491, pp.177, £.9.99
Introduction: Kwame Dawes

Jan Carew, *Black Midas*
ISBN 9781845230951, pp.272 £8.99
Introduction: Kwame Dawes

Jan Carew, *The Wild Coast*
ISBN 9781845231101, pp. 240; £8.99
Introduction: Jeremy Poynting

Austin Clarke, *Amongst Thistles and Thorns*
ISBN 9781845231477, pp.208; £8.99
Introduction: Aaron Kamugisha

Austin Clarke, *Survivors of the Crossing*
Introduction: Aaron Kamugisha
ISBN 9781845231668, pp. 208; £9.99

Neville Dawes, *The Last Enchantment*
ISBN 9781845231170, pp. 332; £9.99
Introduction: Kwame Dawes

Wilson Harris, *Heartland*
ISBN 9781845230968, pp. 104; £7.99
Introduction: Michael Mitchell

Wilson Harris, *The Eye of the Scarecrow*
ISBN 9781845231644, pp. 118, £7.99
Introduction: Michael Mitchell

George Lamming, *Of Age and Innocence*
ISBN 9781845231453, pp. 436, £14.99
Introduction: Jeremy Poynting

Earl Lovelace, *While Gods Are Falling*
ISBN 9781845231484, pp. 258; £10.99
Introduction: J. Dillon Brown

Una Marson, *Selected Poems*
ISBN 9781845231682, pp. 184; £9.99
Introduction: Alison Donnell

Edgar Mittelholzer, *Corentyne Thunder*
ISBN 9781845231118, pp. 242; £8.99
Introduction: Juanita Cox

Edgar Mittelholzer, *A Morning at the Office*
ISBN 9781845230661, pp.210; £9.99
Introduction: Raymond Ramcharitar

Edgar Mittelholzer, *Shadows Move Among Them*
ISBN 9781845230913, pp. 358; £12.99
Introduction: Rupert Roopnaraine

Edgar Mittelholzer, *The Life and Death of Sylvia*
ISBN 9781845231200, pp. 366; £12.99
Introduction: Juanita Cox

Elma Napier, *A Flying Fish Whispered*
ISBN: 9781845231026; pp. 248; £9.99
Introduction: Evelyn O'Callaghan

Orlando Patterson, *The Children of Sisyphus*
ISBN: 9781845230944 ; pp. 220; £9.9
Introduction: Kwame Dawes

Orlando Patterson, *An Absence of Ruins*
ISBN: 9781845231040; pp. 152; £8.99
Introduction: Jeremy Poynting

Andrew Salkey, *Escape to an Autumn Pavement*
ISBN 9781845230982, pp. 220; £8.99
Introduction: Thomas Glave

Andrew Salkey, *Hurricane*
ISBN 9781845231804, pp. 101, £6.99

Andrew Salkey, *Earthquake*
ISBN 9781845231828, pp. 103, £6.99

Andrew Salkey, *Drought*
ISBN 9781845231835, pp. 121, £6.99

Andrew Salkey, *Riot*
ISBN 9781845231811, pp. 174, £7.99

Garth St Omer, *A Room on the Hill*
ISBN 9781845230937, pp. 168, £8.99
Introduction: Jeremy Poynting

Garth St. Omer, *Shades of Grey*
ISBN 9781845230920, pp. 194, £8.99
Introduction: Jeremy Poynting

Garth St Omer, *Nor Any Country*
ISBN 9781845232291, pp. 128, £8.99
Introduction: Jeremy Poynting

Denis Williams, *Other Leopards*
ISBN 9781845230678, pp. 216; £8.99
Introduction: Victor Ramraj

Denis Williams, *The Third Temptation*
ISBN 9781845231163, pp. 108; £8.99
Introduction: Victor Ramraj

Imminent

Roger Mais, *The Hills Were Joyful Together*

V.S. Reid, *New Day*

Michael Gilkes, *Couvade* and *A Pleasant Career*

Wilson Harris, *The Sleepers of Roraima* and *The Age of the Rainmakers*

Garth St Omer, *J—, Black Bam and the Masqueraders*

All Peepal Tree titles are available from the website
www.peepaltreepress.com
with a money back guarantee, secure credit card ordering
and fast delivery throughout the world at cost or less.

Contact us at:
Peepal Tree Press, 17 King's Avenue, Leeds LS6 1QS, UK
Tel: +44 (0) 113 2451703 E-mail: contact@peepaltreepress.com